SILVER & SAGE

SILVER IN THE CITY

A.D. ELLIS

1

BODEN "BODE" SILVER

"I DON'T LIKE HIM. Call the next one on the list." I ran a hand through my messy brown hair before I hefted a moving box onto the kitchen counter and sliced through the packing tape with a box cutter.

"*Bo-dee*," my twin, Benji drew out the syllables of my nickname in a huffy whine, "that was our fifth candidate from the list. He was by far the best of them all." He tapped a pen against the notepad on his lap. We were fraternal twins, but we looked almost exactly the same, enough so that strangers would sometimes confuse us. His hazel eyes snapped to mine. "We *need* a roommate."

He wasn't wrong. This latest guy just wasn't who I wanted to share our apartment with. *Yeah, because one look at him has you all hot and bothered and you'd rather deny him a place to stay than work around any kind of feelings.*

"In all honesty," my cousin, Kyson started, "that's not saying much. The first four applicants royally sucked. This guy, what was his name?"

"Sage," Benji provided.

"Yeah, Sage wasn't just the best of them all, he blew them away." Kyson was not only Benji's and my cousin, but he was our best friend. Born within two months of each other, we were inseparable from birth on. And the family resemblance was uncanny. He could have passed as our brother with no problem. "The first guy looked like he planned to kill us in our sleep."

I couldn't help but smile. He wasn't wrong.

"The girl was fine, seemed cool. But her bestie dropped too many hints about trying to 'convert' us to the hetero side." Benji shook his head. "That third guy almost pissed himself when he learned the apartment was above a bar. When you asked if he was okay with the three of us being gay, I thought he was going to pass out. Probably couldn't pay him enough to take our extra room." Benji laughed.

"Guy number four was already asking about getting an extension on paying rent 'a little late.' That's a hard no." Kyson gave me a look. "Seriously, Bo, Sage seemed great."

"And not just *in comparison*. Sage seemed great overall." Benji stood up. "What could you possibly not like about him?"

"He's a baby, for one." I took plates and cups from the box and began stacking them in the cabinets of the new kitchen. I refused to think about how sweet and innocent the kid looked blushing his way through the applicant interview.

"So, he's young. What did he say? Twenty-four? That's only ten years younger than us." Benji stood with hands on his hips. "Try again. I'm not letting this one slide. What else could you not like about him?"

Kyson left the living room, which was open to the

kitchen, and joined me in unpacking. "He seemed very bright and responsible."

He seemed like a sexy, smart nerd. And I'm not even going to acknowledge why that seems to be a turn on for me.

"He's a student. He needs to study. An apartment above a bar isn't exactly conducive to studying." I broke down one box and opened another one.

"We were very clear with him about the location and probable noise level. He's aware and if he wants the apartment, I don't see why we wouldn't rent to him." Benji continued to stare me down in challenge.

"He was shy and skittish. Not exactly our type." I gave another argument, but I knew it was a lame attempt. "He looked like he thought we were going to eat him alive." *And why the fuck do I keep thinking about wanting to eat him up?*

Benji snorted. "He was definitely intimidated by *you*, but that was probably because you scowled and looked like a fuckin' grump-ass the entire time we talked to him."

"Why are you so against him? He has proof of payment history, references from his old place. Hell, that landlady said she was sad to see him go, but he wants to be closer to downtown. We're on Massachusetts Avenue in downtown Indianapolis. You can't get much closer to downtown. He claims to be tidy, keeps to himself, doesn't care that the room is above a bar, and he was polite. Plus, he was cute." Kyson waggled his brows.

"Soooo cute." Benji smiled. "And was it just me or did he seem super innocent?"

"Yes. Very cute and innocent. Like super smart and capable in so many ways, but fragile and inexperienced in others." Kyson nodded as he broke down another box. "Is that what you're worried about, Bo? This kid is so cute and innocent he may get tarnished by your grumpy gruffness and aversion to relationships?"

My cousin and brother laughed.

I rolled my eyes.

But in all reality, the words hit a little too close to home. Sage was young, innocent, and so damn adorably cute I wanted to wrap him in my arms and protect him. That was a problem. I didn't have time for protecting some kid who I had absolutely nothing in common with. I had a bar to open and make successful. I didn't need a cute nerd as a distraction. But I couldn't very well tell Benji and Kyson that, so I huffed and shrugged.

"Fine. If he wants the room, he can have it. I want it noted that I think he's too young, I think he's not the type for living above a bar, and I think he's going to be more trouble than the rent payment is worth. *And* I'm not taking care of his ass or listening to him gripe and complain about noise level." I unloaded dish soap and sponges to the under-sink cabinet.

"Bode, you've gotta relax. You're tied in knots over The Salty Lizard and it's not even open yet. You're gonna give yourself ulcers." Benji threw an arm over my shoulder.

I was closer to my brother than anyone in the whole world. Together since conception and every day since, we had a special bond. Benji knew me like he knew himself, and I knew him just as well. We were so very similar, but had differences too. I was loud and extroverted, the life of the party, and wanted to prove myself to my father and society. Benji was slightly quieter, preferred to observe the party, and was happy with his art and jewelry creations; he didn't care about proving himself. But Benji had always been my father's *favorite* twin. My dad, Richard—yes, my dad had the perfect porn star name, Dick Silver. And my uncle Rodney was Rod Silver. The guys and I called them the porn brothers—anyway, my dad had always made it clear that I needed to be more like Benji. More studious, not so loud, not so impulsive. So, yeah, I had a lot to prove to my dad with The Salty Lizard.

"I say we contact Sage and offer the room to him. I have a good feeling about him." Kyson held up his phone and raised his brow.

I rolled my eyes. "Fine, offer the room to him." I couldn't help but smile at Kyson's fist pump.

If I was one extreme, Benji was in the middle, and Kyson was the opposite extreme. As a kid, Kyson had always been the most easy-going of the three of us. As an adult, he was the same. He earned his massage therapy license and focused a lot on holistic therapy and healing. Kyson was our ground, our center, our peacemaker. Kyson would be opening his own massage therapy practice soon after The Salty Lizard was opened.

The three of us were born and raised in a small town in southern Indiana. After high school and college, we moved to Indianapolis with our three separate-but-connected goals. Thanks to a loan from Dick Silver, I had money to lease an entire building on Massachusetts Avenue. Downstairs would be The Salty Lizard bar and dance club, and the three of us would live upstairs.

The upstairs apartment was extremely large. It was broken into four separate bedrooms, a kitchen, living room, dining room, and three bathrooms. In order to make paying the lease easier—because most of the loan from my father was going into the bar—the three of us decided that renting out the fourth room would be the best plan. It seemed like Kyson and Benji were set on Sage being our roommate.

As long as the kid didn't bother me, I could deal with it. I had bigger things to worry about. My dad had loaned me the money for the building and getting the bar up and running. He had allowed me one year to prove that I could make The Salty Lizard profitable. But he had promised to check in every month to see where his money was going and if I was using it in ways that he deemed smart and effective.

Dick Silver and Rod Silver were business tycoons in their own right. Dick had started an insurance company and Rod had started an accounting firm in the small town we grew up in. They had no competition when they were first starting out so they quickly had a monopoly on the insurance and accounting needs of our town, our county, and even some of the surrounding towns and counties. Would Richard and Rodney be successful in a large city like Indianapolis? I wasn't sure. They were both good at what they did, but it was hard to say if they would have been as successful in a large market versus the small market they started in. But because they were big fish in a small pond, they had amassed a large fortune both individually and in their shared endeavors.

I was very appreciative of my dad loaning me the money to lease my building and start The Salty Lizard. I did not appreciate the constant pressure and reminders from him about how he was watching to make sure I spent his money the way he deemed fit.

Benji, Kyson, and I had often discussed that our sexuality had never been as much of an issue for our fathers as our future careers. Our moms were best friends and supported us no matter what. Always had and always would. Dick and Rod were more concerned about our financial futures.

Kyson going into massage therapy and planning to make a career out of it in Indianapolis was not only perfect for him, but it meshed well with our fathers' expectations. Kyson was *level-headed* and had a *good head for business* according to Dick and Rod. Kyson would make a great massage therapy practice owner.

Benji had always been passionate about art. He created beautiful pieces of jewelry, decorative artwork as home décor pieces—pottery, paintings, stained glass, and various other mediums—and was planning to combine his love of art and talent in creating pieces with a desire to teach. Soon after The Salty Lizard was up and running, and Kyson's Mass. Ave. Healing Massage was open, Benji would open The Silver Creative. Our dads were just as emphatic that Benji's business was the perfect career for him as they were about Kyson's future practice.

But me? My plan to open The Salty Lizard? Foolish, impulsive, not a sound business decision according to my dad. Uncle Rod was never as hard on me as my dad was, but he did try to sway me toward a different career. No matter that I had the most complete business plan of the three of us. No matter I had taken the most initiative in finding a location—Benji and Kyson had recently found buildings available on Massachusetts, they simply had to wait for some paperwork and finalities to be completed. My dad insisted that a bar and dance club was a waste of time and would be a colossal failure. Would he have said the same if Ky or Benji had planned to open The Salty Lizard?

I sighed. It didn't matter. I was a thousand percent determined to make my business a success. I had the support of my brother and cousin. I had the gumption to make it work. And I had a solid business plan along with a solid financial source. If only my dad would stop lording his power and doubt over my head.

I grabbed three beers from our new refrigerator and took them to Benji and Kyson in the living room. Throwing myself onto the couch I sighed. "Damn, who knew moving could be so exhausting?" I glanced around the room and smiled. "I've got to say I really like this place."

"I agree." Kyson opened his beer and took a long swallow. "I knew I liked it when we first looked at it, but now that everything is moved in I really love it."

Benji opened his beer and threw the cap at me. "The rooms are actually very big. The kitchen and dining room are nice. It's not like we do a lot of cooking for entertaining, so they are perfect for us. The best part is the living room for movies and video games."

I was really looking forward to getting the rest of the boxes unpacked and the apartment organized and decorated. I wasn't much for coordinating colors and decorations, but I knew Kyson and Benji would be all over that shit.

Kyson's phone buzzed. "It's Sage. He wants to know if he can go ahead and move in today."

I glanced at Benji. He shrugged. I sighed. "Sure, tell the kid to come on over."

Kyson tapped out a text with a smile on his face. Benji gave me a stern look.

"You need to go easy on Sage. He seemed quiet and shy, but he seemed particularly nervous around you." My brother never had any qualms about telling me what I should or shouldn't do. Which was fine, because I didn't hesitate to tell him the same.

My face scrunched up. "I'm not going to change who I am because of some innocent little college nerd. If he doesn't like me the way I am, he can lock himself in his room or he can move out. But he loses his first month deposit." I swigged my beer and ignored the little voice inside that told me I was being an asshole douchebag.

Twenty minutes later there was a knock on the door.

"Surely that can't be Sage already." Kyson went to the door. He glanced through the peephole and then turned wide eyes back toward Benji and me. "It's him," he whispered.

Kyson opened the door. "Hey man. Come on in."

Sage stood with a bag on each shoulder, a backpack on his back, and a large box in his hands. His cheeks were pink, and I couldn't tell if it was from the exertion of carrying so much stuff or embarrassment over his excitement to move in. Maybe both.

"I feel kinda silly coming over so quickly." Sage spoke quietly as he stepped through the door. "But I was getting so tired of sleeping on my classmate's couch. Since I gave notice at my old place, I didn't feel it was right to keep staying there. I wanted my old landlady to be able to rent the apartment to someone else as quickly as possible. But sleeping on that couch was getting old."

Benji jumped up and took the box from Sage. "Here let

me help you with that. You can get everything unpacked in your new room."

"Yeah, unpack and then come on out here for our first official house meeting." Kyson gestured towards the living room.

Sage's eyes grew wide, but he nodded before ducking into his room.

"Our first official house meeting? What the hell are you talking about?" I crossed my arms over my chest and scowled at Kyson.

He smiled and spread his arms wide. "We've got this amazing new space, grand new business adventures, and a new friend to share it with. We need to do some bonding and set some ground rules."

"Oh Jesus, Kyson," I growled. "We don't need a bunch of feel-good shit. We've got a new place, we've got new businesses, we've got a new renter. That's all. Don't make this into something that it's not."

Benji took the three empty beer bottles to the kitchen. "No, I think Kyson is right. We need to get to know Sage and he needs to get to know us. After all, we're going to be living together. And it's better to set guidelines and rules now than to argue over them later."

I rolled my eyes and huffed. That was how the three of us worked. Always had been. We were either all in, or two would overrule the third. Looked like this was a *Bode gets overruled* time.

2

SAGE HOLDER

I STOOD in my new room and took a deep breath trying to calm myself. I was a jumble of emotions. Embarrassed about showing up twenty minutes after the guys offered me the room. Excited about having such an amazing space in a gorgeous apartment at a superb location with three of the hottest guys I'd ever laid eyes on. Okay, that last part maybe wasn't so much part of my excitement, but definitely fed into my nerves. Being smart and academically successful with a solid plan for furthering my education definitely didn't help me with being socially awkward and nervous as hell, especially around attractive guys.

"Calm down," I whispered harshly to myself. "They are all older than you. Probably all have significant others and are focused on establishing their careers. None of them are interested in *you*." My mind immediately strayed to Boden Silver. *"Call me Bode or Bo,"* he had said. *"B-o-d-e, but rhymes with Jodie."* Boden, Bode, Bo, I didn't care what he wanted to be called; the man was sex on a stick and made my heart thump out of control. But he was also gruff and seemed intent on making his dislike of me known. I think he was actually disappointed when I said the three of them being gay didn't bother me because I was gay too. Bode had frowned like me being gay was a problem for him.

I chuckled to myself thinking of the phrase *Sometimes truth is stranger than fiction*. Twins and a cousin all gay and they find a gay roommate? I wasn't going to complain; I'd just say a big thank you to Fate. The apartment was too nice, the location too fabulous, and the rent payment too perfect. The fact that I was at least safe from any homophobia while in what was now my home was an amazing bonus. Three hot guys to secretly ogle was icing on the cake.

But I had to put my things away and go face a *house meeting*. With all three of them. Kyson and Benji seemed pretty laid back and nice. Bode seemed like he wanted to chew me up and spit me out. And he did *not* appear to be keen on the idea of a house meeting. The daggers he shot Kyson were proof of that.

I quickly plugged my computer and phone in to charge. Hung some clothes in the closet, grateful for the leftover hangers. Stacked my books on the floor. I left the rest of my clothes in the duffle. First thing I'd need to do was get a bed, a desk, and a dresser. I sighed in relief knowing I had plenty of living expense money left from my grandma. My parents didn't help with a single cent toward my college education. Luckily, I landed multiple scholarships to cover all of my undergrad and graduate degrees. The scholarships covered all expenses of my undergrad education, but the graduate degree scholarships mostly covered only classes, books, and supplies. My adoring grandma had blessed me with a *living expenses allowance* as a gift when she found out I was going on to get my graduate degree. Told me, "You're doing a good thing for your future by furthering your education. No need for you to be broke and suffering in the present if I can help. I can't take the money with me when I go, so I'd rather see it help you now while I'm still around to see it." I loved that woman to the moon and back. I wished she lived closer, but she had moved out to the west coast to live with her sister about a year ago.

I'd saved all of the money she'd been giving me in case of needing to buy bigger items. My last apartment—which was just a room in sweet Mrs. Phegley's house—had come completely furnished. Was it strange I was looking forward to furnishing my own room? I'd gone from living at home with my parents' furniture, to living in a dorm room with stock bunk beds and dressers and desks, to living in a furnished room at Mrs. Phegley's. The thought of picking my own desk, my own dresser, my own bed, maybe even some of my own decorations was exciting. *Damn, man. Chill out. Your inexperience is showing.* It was strange to be twenty-four and at the top of all of my classes academically, yet be such a rookie when it came to having friends and living on my own. Don't get me wrong. I was one hundred percent capable of taking care of myself. But I was an amateur when it came to making and *keeping* friends. Seemed people in my classes only wanted to be my friend if I could help them ace a test. Or they stopped being my friend once they realized I was going to blow them away on every test and assignment. I didn't purposely set out to be the best in every class. I just always seemed to be leaps and bounds ahead of everyone else. My parents seemed to think that made me better than everyone. I looked at it as just a reason for people to not like me.

Once there was nothing else to put away and I'd stalled as long as possible, I took a deep breath and walked out of my room into the living room. My room was toward the back of the apartment, but it was the first room to the right when you came up the main stairs from the back of the bar. A small "public" powder room bathroom was to the left just off the living room where the guys were seated at the moment. The living room was open to the kitchen which then fed into the dining room. Two bedrooms were off to the right and the fourth bedroom was behind the dining room. A second bathroom fit between two of the bedrooms and a third bathroom was shared between my room and the adjoining bedroom.

I gritted my teeth and joined my new roommates in the living room. Kyson and Benji smiled, but Bode's face was a blank slate that I couldn't read as indifference, boredom, or anger. I smiled at everyone and took a seat on the recliner.

"Glad to have you here," Kyson began. "We all voted and you won hands-down over all the other applicants."

Bode cleared his throat.

I got the feeling *he* maybe wasn't as enthusiastic about my arrival.

"You have furniture you need to move in?" Benji asked.

"I was thinking I'd go shopping today and get what I need. My old stuff belonged to my landlady."

"Don't scratch the walls moving things in." Bode had

slouched back on the couch and had his eyes closed with his hands behind his head, elbows out.

Benji started to say something, but I beat him to it.

"Wouldn't dream of it. This place is way too nice to be bumping the walls with a dresser. I'll be careful." I smiled sincerely at Bode when he cracked an eye open to look my way.

He harrumphed and I decided then and there I was going to make the guy like me if it was the last thing I did. Or at least figure out why he *didn't* like me.

"So, you're in college?" Kyson ignored Bode and turned toward me.

"Yeah, I've got my double undergraduate degrees in accounting and finance, and decided to go ahead and get my graduate degree as well. I'm in the Master of Science in Accounting program. Should have my master's degree in accounting in just over two years." I curled my legs up under me and rocked the recliner gently.

"Why not just live on campus?" Bode still had his eyes closed.

"I did for undergrad. My scholarships covered room and board. But it was a different situation for graduate school and I was tired of on-campus living after four years. So, I rented a room with Mrs. Phegley for the last semester of my senior year and this past summer. But I really wanted to be closer to downtown. This place is like a ten-minute bike ride to my classes. So it's perfect."

Bode pursed his lips in a sneer. "Where you planning on keeping a bike?"

Again, Benji started to swoop in to save me, but I just smiled.

"Well, I was thinking I'd be able to keep it out back of

the bar where you three have yours locked up." I didn't purposely bat my lashes, but they may have fluttered a little of their own accord.

Bode actually sat up and scowled at me with his elbows on his knees.

Benji snorted and Kyson coughed.

"Out back is fine." Kyson winked at me.

"Let me make sure I've got this right." I moved to sit cross-legged. "Kyson, you're a massage therapist and will open your practice soon. Benji, you're an artist and will have a store and lessons available soon." I ticked off the men and their jobs on my fingers. "And Bode, you're opening The Salty Lizard downstairs very soon."

Benji and Kyson nodded. Bode crossed his arms over his chest.

"Okay, let's get some house rules set and then Sage can go do his shopping." Kyson grabbed a notepad. "Thoughts on ground rules, guidelines, suggestions?"

"I'm fine with communal food, but if you eat the last of it, replace it." Bode tossed out his idea and gave a slight yawn. "And just be fucking respectful of everyone's food in general."

We all nodded.

"I think being respectful is good overall. Respect your roommates when you're cooking, eating, playing, bringing someone home, that type of thing." Kyson wrote as he spoke.

"Should we do a chore schedule? Assign jobs weekly?" Benji asked.

"Yeah, let's set something up to rotate the chores. Dishes, trash, sweeping, dusting, bathrooms. Bode and Sage can share cleaning their bathroom. Kyson and I will split the cleaning of our bathroom. I'll do the schedule and show you guys for final approval."

"Might be best to have a grocery list we can all add to. Maybe try to do weekly shopping together?" I offered a suggestion. It was difficult trying to fit into this tight-knit group despite Kyson and Benji being so nice.

"Oh, that's good. Actually, I was thinking maybe weekly grocery trip all together and eat out? Sunday mornings maybe?" Kyson glanced around the group. When he didn't get any pushback, he smiled. "Okay, let's plan on that for now."

"I think communication is key. If something is bothering you, speak up. We're all grown-ups," Benji said.

"Mostly." Bode cast a smirk my way.

Benji shot him a look.

Interesting. Did Bode have an issue with my age?

"Okay, okay. Sorry. But, I agree. Communication is key." Bode kicked his feet up on a box in front of his seat on the couch.

"So, we'll have weekly chore rotation, weekly groceries as a group, a weekly meal out where we can have house meetings if needed. Do we want meals here at the house to be set and shared or just whatever and whenever?" Kyson continued taking notes.

"Whatever and whenever sounds easiest. Would be hard to have set and shared meals around four very different schedules." Benji stood and stretched. "Ky, you get that schedule made. I'll put a notepad on the fridge for groceries. Bode, if you're okay with it, I'll just borrow your truck and take Sage furniture shopping."

"The hell you will. No one is driving my truck but me." Bode stood with a frown.

"Well, then I guess you can take Sage furniture shopping." Benji smiled sweetly.

"Oh no, it's okay. I don't want to put anyone out. I'll pay for delivery." I hadn't known Bode had a truck so I wasn't expecting him or the others to help with moving my furniture.

"Nonsense. No reason for you to pay extra when Bode has a truck." Kyson stood from his place on the couch. "Right, Bo?" Kyson might as well have had a cartoon halo over his head for as innocent as he was attempting to come off.

Bode gritted his teeth. "Sure. No problem at all, roomie. But let's get going. I've got stuff to work on in the bar."

I jumped up. "Oh, yeah. Sure thing. And I can help with the bar stuff too. Once we're back. If you want help."

Bode just shrugged. "Get your stuff. Meet me downstairs."

I rushed off to my room and pretended to ignore the heated whispers behind me. I caught bits and pieces of, "…be nice!"

"…am being nice!"

"…looks scared to death of you."

"…so you put him in a truck to go shopping with me?"

"…he's living here, least you can do is be friendly."

"…living here, but doesn't mean the kid has to be my best friend."

By the time I grabbed my phone and wallet, the conversation had died down mostly because Bode had stalked out of the apartment and down the back stairs.

"He'll meet you down at his truck. There's parking behind the building." Kyson gestured toward the back.

"Don't let him bother you. Bode's bark is far worse than his bite. He's a good guy. Really. He's just a little gruff and even more so right now with the stress of opening the bar. It's his baby. He needs The Salty Lizard to be a huge success." Benji put an arm around my shoulders.

"Well, then I guess we all better help him make his baby a success, huh?" I wasn't really sure where the words came from. I moved in here because it was close to school, reasonably priced, and I needed a place to stay. I didn't move in to help grumpy-ass Bode make The Salty Lizard a success. But that was just kinda the vibe I got from the three of them. I may not have been a *part* of them. Yet. But I felt like I already had a place in their group and I wanted to do my part.

Kyson and Benji beamed at me and I blushed before rushing down the stairs to meet Bode.

Why did I feel like a lamb being led to slaughter?

* * *

Bode was in the truck when I got downstairs and I swore he rolled his eyes at me when I climbed in. I chose not to dwell on it.

"Where are you wanting to go?" Bode asked as he pulled the truck out of the parking lot.

"I was thinking about that value furniture place just on the other side of downtown." I glanced at Bode. "But if you'd rather not drive that far we can find something closer."

"Nah, that's fine." Bode pointed the truck for the direction of the store.

We rode in silence for several minutes. It wasn't so much that it was uncomfortable, but I didn't like thinking that Bode was mad at me or didn't like me. My grandma was always using the phrase *in for a penny in for a pound*. I sighed. Looked like it was time to put the phrase to the test.

"Why don't you like me?" I tried not to look at Bode as the words exploded from my mouth, but I caught him staring at me.

He scowled. "It's not so much that I don't like you." The scowl deepened. "I just don't know you very well. Hell, I don't know you at all. It's always just been me, Kyson, and Benji. Just going to take time to get used to having a fourth person around." Bode leaned his left arm against the door of this truck and tapped his right thumb against the steering wheel.

"Well I promise to stay out of the way as much as I can. I'll be studying a lot. I will definitely help with chores. I won't be a bother if you bring a date home or anything like that. And I can help in the bar too." Why was I trying to convince him that I'd be a good roommate? Why did I care if he didn't like me? *You know why. You've always wanted people to like you. You want to keep this apartment. And you think he's hot as hell.*

Bode laughed. "Dude, chill out. The room is yours, you don't have to prove yourself to me."

"Back there it seemed like you wanted me to prove something to you. You've seemed angry with me since the first moment you saw me. I know it shouldn't matter, but it really bothers me when I think people don't like me. And I'd really like to keep this apartment so it would be good if you and I could get along." I chewed on a fingernail and glanced at Bode.

"Don't bite your nails," he commanded. "It's a gross habit. Do you know how many germs are under your fingernails?"

I shivered. "Actually, I do. I've seen the stuff that can grow in petri dishes just from collecting samples from underneath your nails. It's disgusting. Biting my nails is a bad habit. I'm actually trying to quit, but I do it more when I'm nervous."

"Are you nervous now?"

I nodded. "Benji and Kyson don't make me nervous at all. They seem like really nice guys and I think will be good friends."

"But I make you nervous?" Bode glanced my way.

When I nodded, he frowned.

"Sorry about that. I'm under a shit ton of stress from my dad trying to make The Salty Lizard a success. I can't say I'll be a bundle of joy to live with, but I can promise that I don't hate you."

"I guess knowing that you don't hate me will have to be good enough at least for now."

Bode pulled the truck into a parking spot in front of the furniture store.

Before I got out of the truck, I swallowed my nerves. "I really can help with bar stuff, and I wouldn't mind at all if all four of us ended up being friends."

An hour later, Bode and I were sweating our asses off after carrying a bed, a dresser, and a desk up the stairs. I stood in the middle of my room trying to decide where to start with organizing my furniture when I heard Bode curse from the kitchen.

I walked to where he was. "What's wrong?"

He held up a piece of paper. "The guys decided to drive down home to pick up the last of our stuff. They'll be back tomorrow. Which is fine, because the stuff needed picked up. But that leaves me working on bar stuff alone tonight."

"I can help with the bar stuff. I already told you that."

"I thought you had furniture to arrange? And studying to do?"

I shrugged. "I'll help you with bar stuff and you can help me move furniture if I need help later."

Bode stared at me for an uncomfortable amount of time. Finally, he huffed and pointed toward the back stairs. "Fine, I could use the help."

I followed Bode down the stairs and tried to convince myself I wasn't staring at his ass. I'd known I was gay since the very first time my voice broke and probably even before that. I'd been attracted to a lot of guys, but never had a serious relationship. But there was something about the man in front of me, the way his tight ass filled out a pair of jeans, the strength evident in his thighs, the lean muscles in his arms, that had me thinking this was going to be the unrequited attraction that finally did me in. I knew there was no way Bode wanted a relationship with someone so much younger and so much different from him. He was on his way to building his dream career while I still had at least two years of schooling to go. He was outspoken, a people person, and probably the life of the party. I was a quiet, nerdy wallflower. He was gorgeous, I was average. He had promised that he didn't hate me, but that didn't mean he liked me. I would have to settle for being tolerated.

But that didn't mean I wouldn't watch that fine ass every time it walked in front of me.

* * *

"All of those glasses have been washed. They are likely mostly dry, but go ahead and use a cloth to wipe them down before putting them on the shelves. Don't want any spots on them." Bode indicated the shelves I should fill first and then the area where extras would go. As a bar, I assumed The Salty Lizard used *a lot* of glasses.

Bode had music playing while we worked. He appeared to be organizing and inventorying a variety of liquors. The music seemed loud to me, but I assumed it would be much louder once The Salty Lizard was open for business. I should probably prepare for having music as a constant study companion. Or invest in noise-cancelling headphones.

I had an entire row of glasses dried and shelved, I was getting in a groove, and enjoying the music. And then it happened. I wasn't even sure what caused it. One moment, I was kinda bebopping—albeit, awkwardly—around the bar area while drying the glasses and the next moment a glass went flying from my grip and shattered on the floor.

I screamed and lunged as if I'd somehow be able to salvage the glass, but of course it was pointless. I covered my mouth with a hand. "Oh my God, Bode. I'm so sorry."

For the next few moments, we stood staring at the shards of glass covering the bar floor.

Then Bode spent what seemed like an eternity gawking

at me with wide eyes as if he was expecting a film crew to jump out and tell him he'd been Punk'd.

Bode finally broke from his stupor. At first, he looked like he wanted to choke me. Then he gritted his teeth and his nostrils flared. Bode closed his eyes as if he was trying to calm himself by counting to ten.

"I'm sorry. Everything was going great. I don't know how the glass went flying from my hand. I'll pay for it." *Jesus, Sage. You've not even spent one night in your new apartment and you're already fucking up.*

Bode took a deep breath. "Don't sweat it."

I'm not sure if he was trying to convince me or himself.

"It's just a glass." He pinched the bridge of his nose. "How about I show you how to inventory the new shipments?"

I nodded. "I'm sorry, again."

"No worries. It's one glass." Bode showed me to what he referred to as the receiving room. It was stacked with boxes. "You're going to unpack the boxes, check the items off the shipping sheet, enter the item on the inventory spreadsheet, and then stock the shelves."

"It's nothing breakable?" I was only kinda joking.

Bode chuckled and looked at the stacks of boxes. "Tell you what, you stick to this side of the room. The others are liquor, I'll take care of those. The worst you'll be dealing with is toilet paper, napkins, dish soap, and cleaning solution."

I breathed deeply. "I think I can handle that."

Bode winked but then frowned and left the room quickly.

What was with the wink? I wouldn't lie. It went

straight to my dick. But it wasn't like I thought a wink meant anything. Bode didn't need to be upset with himself. *But you know you'll think of that wink nightly for at least a month.* I sighed at the truth my head spoke and started unpacking boxes.

Two hours later, Bode came to the supply room. He whistled. "Damn man, after the unfortunate demise of one of my bar glasses, I had my concerns. But you pulled this shit together like a boss. Awesome." Bode slapped me on the back. "Looks amazing." He picked up the shipping sheets. "Damn man, you got *all* of this checked off, inventoried, and put away?"

I tried to control the beam fighting to fill my face. My cheeks heated. Why was praise from Bode such a turn on? Maybe it meant he didn't think of me as just some little kid. Sure, I was twenty-four, not a *kid*. But compared to Bode's thirty-four, I'm sure I seemed completely immature and inexperienced. "Yeah, once I got into a rhythm, it was smooth sailing." I stacked the last roll of toilet paper on the shelf. "This is definitely something I can help with as needed." I surveyed the shelves. "In fact, I'd kinda like this to be my baby. The thought of someone messing up all my hard work makes me shudder."

Bode laughed. "Deal. Shipping and receiving can definitely be your baby."

We worked to break down boxes for about twenty minutes and put them out back where they'd be picked up with recycling.

"What else needs done?" I stretched my arms over my head and arched my back. I caught Bode's eyes on my waist where my shirt rose to expose skin.

He jerked his gaze away quickly.

Interesting.

Bode coughed. "That's all for tonight. Chairs and tables will be delivered soon. Then we can finalize the layout." He saved the spreadsheet I'd been working in on the computer and put the shipping sheets in a folder. "We need to get a scanner so we can file these things electronically."

"I've got a scanner. It's one of those portable ones. We can use that, no worries." I paused for a moment and frowned. "Sorry, I don't mean to sound like I think I'm part of this business or anything. Just mean you can use the scanner and I'm willing to help out as needed."

Bode rolled his eyes. "I wouldn't *expect* you to help out or be part of the business just because you're living with us. But if you're willing to help, I'm willing to give you a position. Paid, of course." He cocked a brow. "You want it?"

I smiled and nodded. I'd never really *belonged* with a group of people. Now I had a home, people who were like me—at least in some ways—and a job. I didn't expect it to pay a lot, but knowing I had a part in The Salty Lizard gave me a little thrill. "Let me know times you need a hand and I'll work my studying around it."

Bode switched off the light. "Sounds good. Let's go get your furniture moved around."

He was still intimidating. I could tell he still looked at me as just a kid. It was obvious we were about as different as two people could be. But I'd seen a glimpse of another side of Bode and he wasn't *as* scary as I'd thought.

3
___

BODE

HOLY SHIT, Sage was wound tight. The kid needed to learn to loosen up. He didn't seem to know how to have fun and relax. I guess four years of a double major moving straight into a graduate degree probably didn't allow for a lot of fun.

Once we had his desk in the corner he deemed best, we moved the dresser next to the closet and window. Finally, we positioned his bed in the corner of the room that shared a wall with the bathroom door. Plopping the mattress down on the bed, we both groaned in relief after a day of physical labor.

"Test it out." I nodded toward the bed.

Sage blushed.

Damn. That *blush*. If his pale cheeks pinked in such a way, what would the rest of his body look like flushed and heated? *Stop it, Silver. He's a kid. He's your renter. He's going to be an employee. Way too many lines to cross there. Plus, you don't have the time or energy for long-term. Even a hook-up with him is out of the question because he lives with you.*

I crossed my arms and raised my brows to indicate I was waiting on Sage to test out his new bed.

He gave a crooked, shy smile and sat gingerly on the bed. He bounced a bit on the mattress. "It's nice."

I rolled my eyes and huffed. "Get up. Let me show you how it's done."

Sage scrambled from the bed. I didn't want to think about what it did to my dick to consider how much he responded to me. I didn't want the kid being scared of me, but I couldn't deny a certain rush when he seemed so eager to please. *You're fucked in the head, Silver.*

I walked over to his bed, turned my back to it, and flopped down dramatically with my arms spread wide. "Ahhhh, yeah. It's nice. See how it's done? Now your turn."

Sage's cheeks were almost at five-alarm fire level when he bit his lip and walked toward the bed. Turning his back to the mattress, he flopped—okay, maybe not so much *flopped*, but we could work on it—right onto my outstretched arm.

We both froze. *Shit*. The kid was laying on my left arm as we both spread our limbs all over his mattress. If he was a date or a hook-up, the position would be perfect. I'd lift my arm and pull him close to me. He'd roll to his side and cuddle into my chest. But this was *not* a date or a hook-up. My body wanted to wrap my arm around him. My head was screaming to remove myself from the situation. *Danger, danger!*

I sat up quickly. "You want a beer or something? Watch a movie?" Damn, I wished Kyson and Benji were home. I needed a buffer.

"I don't have any studying to do tonight. Yeah, I'll take

a beer." Sage stood up. "I'm going to shower and change first if that's okay. I'm sweaty."

"Yeah, same. You can use the bathroom first. I'm going to order a pizza from down the street. Bazbeaux Pizza, you ever had it?" I pulled my phone from my pocket.

Sage shook his head.

I waved my phone at him. "You're in for a treat. I'll shower after you and then we can walk down to get it." The words were out of my mouth before I knew what I was saying. "I mean, *I* can walk to get it. You don't have to go with me."

"No, that's fine. I'd like to look around. I've been to this part of the city, but never really just to see the sights."

I nodded. *Great. Looks like the two of you are walking to get pizza. Together. Me and my damn mouth.*

Sage grabbed some clothes and went into our shared bathroom before I left his room and made the call to order pizza.

I walked into my room and closed the door. Perhaps it was the change in pressure. Perhaps it was a faulty latch. Perhaps it was a damn fairy godmother granting me unspoken wishes. Either way, that was the evening I got an eye full of Sage Holder as he climbed from his incredibly quick shower. The door was barely cracked. I should have looked away. Walked away. Instead, I stood with my heart pounding in my chest and my dick throbbing in my pants and watched Sage dry himself. Gawked at the light brown hair that dusted his chest and trailed to his cock. Nearly swallowed my tongue as Sage stroked his plump dick once, twice, three times before pulling on a pair of boxer briefs. I marched my damn voyeur ass from my room and palmed my own dick. *Fuck.* I would *not* think about what had Sage hard. I would *not* think about the fact that he'd been with me all day and now was alone in the apartment with only me. I would *not* consider that maybe *I* was what had him hard. Fuck no. I wasn't letting my head—or my dick—go there.

Sage exited his room in a pair of well-worn sweatpants and a baby blue t-shirt. "Shower's all yours." He slid a pair of dark-rimmed glasses onto his face and they immediately fogged up from the heat of his skin.

I gave a quick nod and all but ran to my room. I took a shower in as cold of water as I could manage and willed my dick to calm the fuck down. Ten minutes later I ran a towel through my damp hair and pulled on a pair of basketball shorts and a gray shirt. I found Sage sitting on the couch. He glanced up when I walked out of my room.

"Ready?" I grabbed my house key and shoved it in my pocket as I slid on some shoes.

Sage did the same and we ambled down the stairs.

Bazbeaux Pizza was a short walk down Mass. Ave. "That building over there is the one that Benji is hoping will be his art and jewelry store. Just waiting on all the paperwork to be finalized." I pointed to an empty storefront.

We grabbed the pizza and headed back to the apartment. I gestured a few buildings down from The Salty Lizard. "See that building that looks a little newer? That's where Kyson's massage therapy place will be."

Sage nodded. "Did you guys plan for all your businesses to be on the same street?"

I shrugged. "Kinda. I mean, it was a goal. But we knew it maybe wouldn't happen that way. Really lucked out that we found the perfect buildings so close together."

We went around the back of our building and tramped up the stairs.

"You still want that beer or you want a pop?" I opened the fridge.

"Pop?" Sage scoffed. "If you mean *soda*, yes, I'll take a soda."

I pursed my lips. "Pop, soda, Coke, same thing."

"I hate the word *pop*. And Coke is only one brand; not all caffeinated sodas are *Coke*. Soda is the appropriate word." Sage pulled two paper plates from a package in the pantry.

I rolled my eyes. "Whatever, smarty-pants. Would you like a *soda*? I've got Pepsi, Coke, Sprite, and Dr. Pepper."

"Yes, please. Dr. Pepper." Sage ripped two paper towels from the roll. "I actually don't really like beer that much."

He followed me to the living room. I placed the cans of pop and pizza box on the coffee table and Sage added the paper plates and napkins.

"Then why did you say you'd take a beer?" I dropped to the couch and opened the pizza box.

Sage blushed and shrugged. "You offered it, I didn't want to be rude."

I raised a brow. "If some guy offers you cocaine, you gonna snort it just so you don't seem rude? Some creep offers to take you back to his place and you're not comfortable, you say yes just so you don't seem rude?"

Sage scrunched his face. "No, not with those things. I mean, I'm not usually around people who would offer me cocaine. And no one offers to take me back to his place, creep or not. I wouldn't be stupid or unsafe in those situations."

"But you'd take a beer from me just because you don't

want to tell me no?" I frowned. "That's not cool. I'm sorry if I came across like I was pressuring you. You tell me no. You tell Ky and Benji no. You tell *anyone* no if you're not into it or uncomfortable. You hear me?" I felt like a damn father handing down advice to a child.

"You didn't pressure me. I wasn't uncomfortable. I don't *hate* beer; drinking one with a new friend wasn't going to put me in a bad situation. I'd just prefer soda with pizza." Sage pulled off his glasses and wiped them on his shirt. "I know I'm not nearly as socially adept as I am academically, but I wouldn't give in to peer pressure if it was completely against my wishes or put me in a bad position."

I took a bite of pizza and savored it for a moment. "You seem almost genius-level smart, I've caught onto that. You don't feel as comfortable socially as you do academically?"

"Heck, no." Sage bit into the pizza and groaned. "This *is* good." He swallowed his bite. "I can run circles around almost any academic topic. But put me in a social situation and I'm sure to flounder. I've found if I'm *too* smart, people don't like me. I struggle with small talk. I stumble over words and feel dumb. I don't often have a lot in common with people."

"So, we're basically exact opposites." I smiled around another bite of pizza. "Not only are we strikingly different physically," I started but stopped when Sage's face fell. "Stop that. I'm not saying it in a bad way. Just look at us. We're like a study in contrasts. I'm taller, you're shorter. My hair is darker, yours is lighter. Our eyes are completely different." I wanted to mention that his body was slight, looked soft, seemed fragile. But I feared that point of contrast would come across as offensive. "And then there's the non-physical differences. You're a genius, I barely made it through school. You're shy and quiet. I love shootin' the shit with friends and strangers. Love to make the rounds at a party."

"God, that sounds like a nightmare." Sage shuddered.

I laughed. "You don't like parties?"

He shrugged. "I guess I wouldn't mind being at a party with people I like. I just don't like going to a party and knowing no one. I just end up in a corner and leaving early."

I studied him for a while. "Thing is, I may chat people up, but I don't get too close. I bet you make real connections."

Sage shook his head. "Not really. I can't really say I have many friends. Connections are hard."

My heart hurt for the kid. "Well, working down at the bar should help you work on the social skills." I wiped my mouth and took a swig of my pop. "And you've got three built-in friends now. Maybe it will all get easier over time."

I swear the kid looked at me like he was going to cry.

I tossed another piece of pizza on his plate. "Told you it was good pizza. Eat up."

Fifteen minutes later, I kicked up my feet on the coffee table. "Wanna play a game?"

Sage frowned. "Let's clean up this mess first."

"Nah, leave it."

"No. That's just gross. You're a grown-up, shouldn't you be living like one and not like a frat boy?" Sage stood with his hands on his hips. "Seriously, Bode, you want to be seen as a professional business owner? Don't leave leftover pizza and trash sitting in the living room."

I stared at the bossy little shit for a moment. *God damn it. I don't need this shit. Don't need some college kid telling me how to live my life.* But his damn words rang in my head. Fuck. He was right. "Ya know, when I told you to speak up, I didn't mean you had to be such a bitch about it." I huffed and stood from the couch to clean up the mess. "You're a damn ball-buster."

Sage just smirked. "Maybe you'll teach me social skills and I'll teach you how to be a real grown-up who cleans up after himself." He followed me to the kitchen and put the remaining pizza in a plastic container.

"Teach me to be a real grown-up?" I growled. "It's not like I would have left it there. I just wanted to play a game first."

"Responsibilities first, fun later."

I sighed. "Don't you need to go study?"

Sage smiled sweetly. "No. I'm good. Let's play that game."

After ten minutes of NBA 2K20, I realized that Sage wasn't into sports games.

"You have no issues telling me to clean up my dinner, but you can't tell me that you don't like basketball games?"

Sage shrugged. "It's not so much that I don't *like* them, I'm just not super good at them. I prefer fighting games. Mortal Kombat is more my thing."

I pressed my lips together. "Yeah, I'm more into the sporting games. Don't have that one."

"If I can set up my system, we can play it. It's a lot of fun." Sage raised his brow.

Damn kid looked like a five-year-old wanting to show his big brother a new game. *Shit*. "Yeah, go ahead. Get it set up. I'm going to the bathroom."

By the time I returned, Sage had set up his PlayStation 4 next to my Xbox One and had Mortal Kombat ready to play.

We spent the next hour playing. It was definitely Sage's type of game and I sucked at it. Hard. I didn't dislike the game, just hated how bad I was at it. But we chatted back and forth the whole time. We pretty much agreed on *nothing*, but Sage seemed more open and comfortable when he had something to occupy his mind while he talked.

Favorite ice cream?
    Me, mint chocolate chip.
    Sage, strawberry.

Favorite season?
    Me, summer.
    Sage, fall.

Favorite video game system?
    Me, Xbox.
    Sage, PlayStation.

Morning or night?
    Me, night.

Sage, morning.

Favorite sport?
    Me, football.
    Sage, doesn't follow sports.

Favorite book?
    Me, doesn't read.
    Sage, can't pick just one.

Favorite food?
    Me, pizza.
    Sage, stir fry.

Favorite outside activity?
    Me, hiking.
    Sage, biking.

Rollercoasters?
    Me, hell yes.
    Sage, only if forced to.

Favorite dessert?
    Me, anything chocolate.
    Sage, doesn't love sweets.

·   ·   ·

Favorite types of movies?

Me, action and comedy.

Sage, sci-fi and comedy.

"Whoa! We finally got something similar. Okay, comedy movies are on the agenda. The guys like those too." I wasn't sure why it seemed important to find *something* we had in common. "We really are about as different as they come, aren't we?"

Sage glanced my way and smiled. "Yeah, but different isn't bad. It would be boring if we were all the exact same. Are you and Kyson super similar? You and Benji?"

I laughed. I was so focused on all of the differences between Sage and me. But in reality, my brother and cousin and I were very different. I mean, we had more similarities than Sage and me, but we had very different personalities and talents. "Kyson is all peace and love and healing with touch and natural means. I'm more about showing people a good time. Benji is one of the most talented artists I've ever seen. He's patient and puts his whole self into his work. He's amazing. I can't draw a stick figure. But the three of us know each other so well, we can almost read each other's minds."

Sage listened intently and then smiled softly. "That sounds wonderful. Best friends, brothers, cousins, so similar yet so unique. I'd love to have connections like that."

"You'll get there. You're young. Maybe having us around will help." I continued to suck at the game, but kept playing so we could keep talking. "What's the craziest thing you've ever done?"

Sage kept his eyes glued to the screen, but bit his lip as he thought about my question. "Um, I skipped class once my senior year of college."

I waited for him to laugh or make a joke. The kid was dead serious. "The craziest thing you've ever done was skip one college class?" *Holy shit*.

"Well, yeah. Skipping class just isn't my thing. I felt guilty all day."

"So, you've never gone skinny dipping? Had sex in public? Made prank phone calls? Ran a red light?" I rambled off things that seemed simple.

Sage shook his head and chewed the inside of his cheek. "None of those. Couple of them sound fun, though." His face flamed and he dipped his head as if trying to hide from his words.

My dick pulsed and I swallowed thickly. "Keep the red light running to a minimum. It's not safe." That's all I could come up with.

"Yeah, true." Sage paused the game. "Thanks for playing. I think I'm going to read and go to bed." He rushed from the room.

I sat in the living room and stared at the ceiling for twenty minutes. *Fuck. What the hell was that?* Did Sage mean the skinny dipping or public sex? He was so innocent, maybe he just meant the prank call?

I finally headed down to the bar and unloaded the rest of the liquor. An hour later, I wandered upstairs and went to bed. I wasn't sure how long I laid there until I eventually drifted to sleep.

4
———

SAGE

SHIT.

Shit. Shit. Shit.

I may as well have just announced to Bode that I was an inexperienced—in every sense of the word—nerd who had no friends and didn't know how to have fun.

Sure, I'd never done any of those things. Some by choice, some because the opportunity had never presented itself. But instead of playing it cool, maybe holding my cards close to the chest, I got tripped up over the thought of skinny dipping. With Bode. Or public sex. With Bode. And I'd blurted out that his suggestions sounded fun.

I took a deep breath and ran my fingers through my hair. It wasn't as if I'd said *which* of the items sounded fun. Maybe he thought I meant running a red light or making a prank phone call. *Or he thought you're a loser for never going swimming naked or having sex in a public place.*

I frowned. No, Bode didn't seem to be the type to think I was a *loser* for not doing those things. In fact, earlier he was doling out advice in an almost parental way.

He seemed to want me to stand up for myself and do what was best for me. He may have been surprised to find out I hadn't done a lot of crazy things, but I didn't think he'd judge me for it.

Flopping down on my bed—in as close to the way as Bode had demonstrated—I immediately regretted it. Not only was I thinking of Bode as a parental figure, I recalled laying close to him on my bed, his arm under my back. I was an idiot to think he'd ever want to move that arm and pull me close to his side. Some guy who looked at me as a kid, gave parent-like advice, and saw me as nothing more than a studious and inexperienced interruption to his life wasn't going to give a second thought to me in any type of sexual way.

I shifted on the bed, slipped my glasses from my face and laid them on the headboard, and began a war with my head trying to fall asleep.

* * *

A week later, I was relieved to have finished a project and a test in a summer class. Bode was just a few days from the grand opening of The Salty Lizard. And the tension between us had been thick. Benji and Kyson were great buffers, but it didn't keep us from butting heads.

I was usually awake early. Bode usually slept in. That caused an issue with the bathroom. In a way, it was nice because we almost never tried to use our shared bathroom at the same time. I annoyed Bode with early morning showers. Bode annoyed me with late night showers.

Bode never hung his towel up and left his clothes on

the bathroom floor. He didn't like it when I threw his belongings into his room.

"Do you really need to open my door at the ass crack of dawn every damn morning to give me my clothes?" Bode grumped from under his blanket one morning.

"I wouldn't have to if you'd take your things from the bathroom with you. And maybe hang a towel up on occasion?"

An hour later, Bode emerged from his room with a scowl. "I thought you finished class? Didn't you want to sleep in just a little?"

I took a bite of toast. "My internal clock just wakes me up. No reason to laze in bed if I'm awake. No one said you had to get up."

Bode and I had, despite our rubbing each other the wrong way most of the time, fallen into a pretty solid routine with both our time and our nit-picking. He pushed, I pushed back. I poked, he poked back. It was somewhat irritating, but it wasn't uncomfortable. If I was honest, I'd miss our daily bickering about menial things.

"Good morning!" Benji announced as he came into the kitchen with Kyson behind him. "We have a plan."

Bode groaned. "Oh Lord. That's scary."

"It's a good plan." Kyson smiled as he headed to the refrigerator.

"It's time for a family vacation." Benji leaned against the counter. "Maybe more along the lines of a road trip. Bode, you need a breather from planning the opening. You've got everything set."

I nodded. It sounded like a good idea. "Bode, you really do have the bar completely set up and ready. You've covered every single thing. Take a break."

"Exactly!" Kyson jumped in. "And Sage is finished with his test and project."

I glanced around the room, confused. "Um, yeah. Since I'm finished, I can take care of things around here while you're gone." Was that what he was getting at?

Benji snorted. "No, Sage. We don't want you to stay here to collect our mail and water the plants."

I waited for the punchline.

"We want you to go *with* us." Kyson spoke slowly.

"Why?" I couldn't control the scrunch of my face.

Benji laughed. "Because you're our roommate and friend. You're kinda part of the package now."

My heart skipped a beat. As in I think it literally stopped for a moment. "You guys want me to go on a road trip. With you. *All* of you."

Bode chuckled, put his hands on my shoulders from behind, and gave me a shake. "Close your mouth, you'll catch flies. No reason to argue with them or doubt them. If they've made up their mind, it's all over. Looks like we're going on a road trip." He didn't let his hands linger despite how much I would have liked him to. "Where are we going? I'm all for a breather even if you have to force me into it."

"Going down home. Spend some time with family. Enjoy the small-town life. Bonfire, four-wheelers, wiener roast, drinking." Benji opened a box of cereal and poured some into a bowl.

"So basically, reliving high school." Kyson poured a glass of orange juice.

"Sounds good. Nice little last hurrah before we get the Lizard up and running. I'm in." Bode sipped a cup of coffee.

The three men turned to look at me.

My mouth opened and closed like a dying fish. *Why would you want me with you?* But I swallowed the words and smiled. "When do we leave?"

Kyson and Benji whooped. Bode just rolled his eyes, but at least he wasn't scowling.

We made plans to leave the next morning. Bode, Kyson, and Benji went down to work in the bar. I needed to ride over to campus for a bit, but I promised to come assist at the Lizard when I got back.

Once I returned from campus, I parked my bike out back and meandered to the front of the building since I knew the back door was crowded with boxes. My first job would likely be to clear the new shipments.

When I reached the front, I saw a man and little boy sitting on a bench. The little boy licked a dripping ice cream cone while the man smiled down at him. I gave a smile and small wave as I turned the corner to approach the Lizard.

"You the owner?" the man asked.

His question caught me by surprise and I stuttered to a stop. "Huh? Oh, me? No. I live upstairs with the owner, but I just help out from time to time." I wondered if it sounded weird to say I lived with the owner. "I'm just a renter with the owner and his brother and cousin."

The man stood and held out a hand. "I'm Bay Whitfield. I own the motorcycle shop a few blocks over, but I just moved into an apartment here on Mass. Ave. This is my son, Arlo."

The little boy gave me a sloppy smile as he continued to lick his treat.

"Nice to meet you." I held out my hand. "I'm Sage Holden."

"So, when does the place open?" Bay gestured toward the bar.

"Just under a week." This was the point in casual chit chat where I usually got awkward and stumbled over my words.

"This may be a stretch, but do you know of anyone reliable who does any baby-sitting? I just recently got custody of Arlo and I'm trying to line up childcare for times when he's not at school or I can't watch him." Bay appeared to be close to fifty and Arlo was little, maybe under five. "He'll be in school during the week. My mom can help on weekends. But I'm looking for someone who can help on an occasional afternoon or weeknight. He can hang at the shop with me most of the time."

"I don't know anyone off the top of my head, but come in and meet the guys. They may know someone." I opened the front door and waited for Bay and Arlo to walk through.

Kyson, Benji, and Bode were sitting at the bar.

"Hey, guys, this is Bay Whitfield and his son, Arlo. He's needing someone to watch Arlo from time to time on afternoons or evenings."

Bay stepped forward to shake my roommates' hands as they introduced themselves. Benji and Kyson gave friendly smiles. Bode looked like he wanted to punch Bay. *What the hell?*

"You live around here?" Bode asked as he tapped his fingers on the bar.

"Yeah, here on Mass. Ave. I own the motorcycle shop a few blocks over. Whitfield's Motorcycle Sales and Service." Bay ruffled Arlo's hair. "My sister passed away recently and she left custody of Arlo to me."

Bode at least had the decency to smile kindly at the little boy before returning to grilling Bay. "No friends, girlfriends, boyfriends, family to watch your kid?"

"Bode!" Benji interjected.

Bay faced Bode squarely and it seemed like they were about to throw down. "Not that it's any of your business, but my mom is able to help on the weekends. The guys who work for me are great but maybe not suited for baby-sitting. And I currently don't have a boyfriend. If and when I'm looking for one, my type is *not an asshole*."

Kyson snorted and gave Bay a shy smile.

Benji grinned.

Bode huffed.

"You know, I don't have tons of experience with kids, but I'm willing to watch Arlo as needed. He can come here or I can come to your place." The words spilled out before I really even knew what I was saying. Arlo was a cute kid. How much trouble could he be?

Bay took Arlo's soggy ice cream cone as Kyson grabbed a napkin for the kid.

Bode jerked his head my way. "You're going to go to a complete stranger's house and watch his kid?"

"Maybe you could come over for a few playdates to get to know us first?" Bay wiped Arlo's messy face.

"Playdates?" Bode sneered. "Get to know *us*?"

Bay and I spoke as if Bode wasn't standing there gawking and being rude.

"That sounds good. I'm sure I can play with a little

kid." I shot Bode a look. I wasn't sure why he was being such a prick.

"Sometimes he's happy with just a movie." Bay wadded up the napkin. "Could he use the bathroom before we walk back home?"

Bode rolled his eyes at Bay, but looked down at Arlo. "Hey, buddy. Follow me."

Bode turned toward the bathroom. Arlo and Bay followed.

By the time they returned, Bay was smirking and Bode may as well have had steam pouring from his ears for as irked as he looked.

Bay and I exchanged phone numbers so we could set up a time for me to go play with Arlo.

"You know, if Sage isn't available, I'm sure Benji and I could keep a kid entertained for a few hours if you'd like. The jury is still out on Bode." Kyson winked and held out his hand for Bay's phone. "I'll give you our numbers in case you can't get ahold of Sage."

Bode grabbed a towel and began cleaning a spotless bar as he glowered at the four of us. When Bay asked Arlo if he was ready to leave, Bode came around the counter to kneel down and talk to the little boy.

I wasn't sure what was said between them, but Arlo smiled and gave Bode a high five. My heart fluttered as I observed such a soft side of Bode when he'd appeared to be purposely rude to Bay.

Kyson cleared his throat. "Um, I'll walk you to the door. I've got some errands to run down the street anyway."

Bode, Benji, and I all glanced at each other. What *errands* did Kyson have? When Bode and Benji chuckled knowingly, I felt my cheeks heat. *Duh.* Kyson maybe had a tiny *crush-at-first-sight* on Bay.

"Kyson loves him an older guy." Bode shook his head as his cousin sauntered away.

"Silver and the fox," Benji played on their last name and Bay's age.

"Bay *is* extremely attractive," I mused as I watched Kyson and Bay out the window. "I mean, for his age."

Bode gave a growly groan and marched toward the back room. "You've got a bunch of receiving to do in the back if you can stop drooling over a man twice your age."

I rolled my eyes and followed him. "I'm not *drooling.* I said he was attractive. Besides, I think Kyson may have just called dibs."

Bode grumbled something about "old enough to be your father" before opening the laptop searching for the receiving file. "Since you've got your own little routine back here, I'll leave you to it. Holler if you need help. Try not to break anything." He walked to the door, but turned back to face me with a scowl on his face. "Thanks for your help. I've been logging your hours, you'll get paid in the first round of payroll after the official opening."

"No worries. I know where you live. I can pester the shit out of you if you don't pay me." I grabbed a box cutter and started opening boxes as Bode turned again to leave.

5

———

BODE

MY BODY WAS a mass of tension.

Who the fuck did Bay Whitfield think he was? I clenched my fists as I recalled our private conversation when the little boy needed the bathroom.

I gestured toward one of two unisex bathrooms.

Arlo announced, "I pee by self" and marched into the restroom.

Bay stood at the door with his foot holding it open so he could keep an ear on his child. He cocked his head and gave me the once over. "You've got it bad, huh?"

"Got what bad?" I crossed my arms. I wasn't sure why I didn't like the guy. Maybe it had something to do with the fact that I wondered if he liked Sage. Or if Sage liked him. True, I hadn't liked Sage upon our first meeting either. Did I like Sage now or did I just tolerate him?

"Got it bad for Sage."

I snorted. "Not likely. He's a roommate, a renter, and an employee. And if you didn't notice, he's too young for me." I knew I was being an asshole, but I leaned in closer. "So, he's clearly way

too young for you." Bay was probably close to fifty. No way he
needed anything to do with Sage.

It was Bay's turn to snort. "I like 'em young, but not that
young. But you keep feeding yourself those excuses if that's what
you need."

"Not excuses, they're facts."

"Doesn't change the fact that you're hot for him." Bay
shrugged as Arlo flushed the toilet. "If it helps, I'm about a
thousand percent sure he's got it bad for you too."

"We're about as opposite as they come. But you go ahead and
spin your little stories." I stepped closer so I could speak quietly
while Arlo happily played at the sink. "He's a new friend, but he's
one of us. I swear to God, if this baby-sitting gig is just a ruse to
get in his pants, I will end you if you hurt him."

Bay laughed. The asshole laughed. "Man, I don't want in his
pants. But that's clearly something on your mind. Don't lose your
chance with him. He seems smart and sweet. Don't mess up. He
has that innocent air about him. You going to be the one to show
him the world? Or watch him with someone else? Lots on the line.
No pressure." He waggled his brow and stepped into the bathroom
to help Arlo speed up his hand washing.

I was left with a simmering anger and a more intense dislike of
the man.

I slammed a glass a little too hard as I put it away as I
thought of the conversation between me and Bay. Kyson
glanced my way with a frown as he returned from outside.

"Man, what's your deal? You look like you're ready to
spit nails." Benji was placing drink menu specials in card
holders on tables.

"Just wondering why everyone was falling all over
themselves with Bay. Seemed like an asshole to me. You
think he's got a thing for Sage?" My brows drew together.

"You mean because he was looking for someone to watch his new son and asked Sage for suggestions?" Benji tapped his chin. "Yeah, probably just an elaborate scheme to get to Sage."

"I'm guessing he's been staking out the joint, watching Sage, spinning a story about how he needs a baby-sitter. Then just sat out front feeding Arlo ice cream cones until Sage came around the corner." Kyson pursed his lips and nodded, completely straight-faced.

I rolled my eyes.

"What did he say to you back there?" Benji gestured toward the bathroom.

I shook my head. But Benji and Kyson both just waited. "Fuck. Nosy asshole is what he is. Told me I had it bad for Sage. And that pressure was on me to do right by him or watch him with someone else. Said Sage liked me too." I pinched the bridge of my nose. "As if, right? The kid—and *kid* is a very operative word—is way too young, a renter, and an employee."

My damn brother and cousin glanced at each other and smirked before turning toward me and fucking grinning like fools.

"What the fuck are you two smiling about?"

"Look, we were going to give it a little more time, but since you brought it up..." Benji started.

"I didn't bring anything up. Bay brought it up and you two made me tell you." I crossed my arms over my chest.

"We have a few thoughts." Benji pulled a chair out and motioned for Kyson and I to sit.

I sighed. "Of course, you do." I plopped in the chair as Kyson patted my shoulder and sat next to me.

"First thought is you need to back off of Sage. You

don't have to be so grumpy and gruff and nit-picky. You two bicker like grumpy old men." Kyson played with the salt and pepper shakers.

"Second thought is, despite you thinking he's too young or any of those other excuses, you *do* seem to have it bad for him. And I'd agree that he's got it bad for you. You two go back and forth like you don't like each other, but the looks in your eyes prove you wrong." Benji tapped his fingers on the table.

"You're both morons. Go ahead and believe what you want to. He's a kid. He's still in school. He and I have almost nothing in common. I'm his landlord. And now I'm his employer. Not a single one of those things is a good idea in a relationship." I leaned back in my chair.

"He's twenty-four years old. That's not a kid. He's only ten years younger than you. He's in school because he's smart and he has plans for his future. You don't have to have a lot in common to find someone attractive. Stop saying you're his landlord like it's something dirty. He lives with us and pays rent the same as we do. None of those things should stop you if you want to pursue things. He wasn't your employee when you first found him attractive. You didn't give him the job because you find him attractive. Did you?" Benji drew designs with his finger on the table.

"Of course not." I scowled. "I gave him the job because he's amazing at tracking and organizing the supplies."

"We just think that you should be a little more open-minded. Maybe admit that you like him and see where things go. He may not even want a relationship. You both can take things slow, just see how it goes." Kyson stacked the salt and pepper shakers on top of each other.

"Whatever. What if I admit I like him and he doesn't feel the same? Would he want to move out? What if we give it a try and it crashes and burns? We lose a renter. You guys said he was the best of all the applicants. I'm not taking a risk of losing a good roommate. Do I think he's fucking adorable and gorgeous? How could I not? That doesn't mean I'm going to lose his rent payment or his help here in the bar. You guys go ahead and believe what you want to believe. Yes, he's cute as fuck. But there's nothing between us and that's the way it has to stay." I stood up from the table. "I'm going to finish up out here and then check to see if Sage needs any help. What time do you want to leave in the morning?"

Benji and Kyson both rolled their eyes at being dismissed. We decided on a nine o'clock in the morning departure time. My cousin and brother went to work finalizing the décor while I stalled for time with every last job I could think of up front. When I had no choice, I headed to the back to check on Sage.

Damn my brother and cousin, and Bay for putting thoughts in my head. Damn them for making me wonder if Sage found me attractive. Damn them all.

* * *

The next morning, armed with coffee and hot tea, the four of us threw our bags in the trunk and piled in Benji's car. I called shotgun, so Kyson and Sage were in the backseat. I hated sitting in the back, and I didn't need to be stuck back there with Sage for the whole trip.

The drive was only about two and a half hours, but we had planned to stop at a state park and do some hiking.

Twenty-five minutes into our drive, Benji pulled into a gas station.

"Time for fuel and snacks!" I jumped from the car.

Once inside the store, I noticed Sage looked a little lost. "You don't want any road trip snacks?"

Sage shrugged. "I'm not real experienced with road trips. Do we just pick foods that we like?"

My heart hurt. This beautiful boy, this damn genius with the sweet heart, had never been included in a road trip. "Yep, drinks, snacks, candy, anything you think you want on the drive." I watched Sage tentatively grab a candy bar, chips, and a drink. I purposely threw extra candy, extra chips, and an extra drink in my basket just for Sage.

Back in the car, Benji announced it was game time. "So, *Never Have I Ever* is difficult to play if you're not drinking. Plus, we don't need ten restroom breaks. *Truth or Dare* is hard in the car if you choose dare. So, we're going to play a combo of the two. When it's your turn, you state something you've done or not done, and the other players have to truthfully tell their experience. You all in?"

I shrugged. "Sure." Benji always thought a road trip needed a damn game.

Kyson and Sage agreed to the game.

"Okay, I'll start." Benji paused to think while he switched lanes to merge into traffic. "We'll start easy, but I think the rule is we can get as in-depth as we want."

I glanced over my shoulder and caught a glimpse of Sage taking a drink. His eyes went wide and his cheeks pinked deliciously. Oh, the things I wanted to hear the kid admit.

"I have seen every episode of *Glee*." Benji stated his truth and looked to me.

I rolled my eyes. "I've seen every episode because you made me watch it."

Kyson chuckled. "Same. But I actually enjoyed it. Not sure Bo did."

Sage smiled. "I stopped watching on the last season. Got bored. In my defense, a roommate watched it, so that's why I watched."

"Your turn, Bode." Benji tapped his fingers on the steering wheel.

I thought over my question. I could go straight for the jugular, but I didn't want to set Sage on edge. I already knew he'd never skinny dipped, run a red light, or made a prank call. I decided my first question would be easy. "I've jacked off in bed while someone else was in the room sleeping."

"Oh, don't I fuckin' know it." Benji laughed and groaned. "I don't know if you were *trying* to be quiet. If so, you sucked at it."

I laughed. Benji and I had shared a room most of our lives even through college. I knew he'd heard me. But if you can't share that with your twin do you even really have a relationship? Actually, that gave me a great idea for my next question.

"Don't act like you didn't do the exact same thing." I smacked the back of my hand against Benji's arm.

"Fine. I did the same thing. But I think I was a lot quieter."

I snorted. "What about you, Ky?"

"I have jacked off in bed with a boyfriend sleeping next to me. Worked out well. He woke, realized what I was doing, and helped me finish things." Kyson shifted in the back seat. "We broke up, but that was a fun time."

I turned to Sage. "Your turn."

Sage's face was as red as a tomato. "I've never shared a room with anyone. Never really had anyone sleeping in my bed. The most I've done is jack off while my parents or Mrs. Phegley were in the same house. With my door locked."

I immediately wanted to sleep in Sage's bed and wake to hear him stroking himself. *Fuck*. These damn thoughts were getting out of control. It was all Benji, Kyson, and *Bay's* fault. I swallowed hard. "Kyson. You're up."

Kyson rubbed his hands together and laughed evilly. "I've recently or currently had a crush on someone older than me."

I glared at Kyson by way of the side mirror, but the fucker just winked.

"Would the most recent someone be named Bay?" Benji teased.

"Maybe, maybe not. That's my truth. I don't have to give specifics." Kyson kicked the back of my seat. "Bode?"

I wanted to growl and pout and refuse to answer. "I've not recently had a crush on anyone older than me." Like Kyson, I wasn't giving specifics. And whatever my fucking head was going on and on about with Sage wasn't *a crush*. It wasn't. I found him attractive. That's it.

Benji laughed out loud. "Hmmm, I think I just decided on my next question."

I shot him a *I'll kill you* look.

"Fine, fine. I have not *recently* had a crush on someone older than me. But in high school, I crushed hard on a

Senior when I was a gangly, gawky Freshman. What about you, Sage?"

The kid could lie. Any of his answers could be fabrications. But something told me he wasn't the type to be deceitful.

"I have recently or currently had a crush on someone older than me." His words rushed from his mouth before he took a gulp of his drink. "Okay, my question."

The way he changed the subject as quickly as possible made me wonder who his crush was on. And the thought that it might be me went straight to my dick.

Sage cleared his throat. "I knew I was gay right about the time I hit puberty. I found a stack of Playboy and Playgirl magazines in the attic of a house I was helping to clean. The Playboy icked me out. But the Playgirl? I didn't understand why or what it meant at the time, but I couldn't take my eyes off the men." After Sage's word vomit, he clapped a hand to his mouth.

I was turned in my seat so I could see him and I had to take pity on the kid as his ears turned so red they looked as if they'd catch his hair on fire. I cleared my throat. "I'm going to take everyone's answer on this one." Kyson and Benji chuckled, but allowed me to keep speaking. "The three of us knew we were gay when we were about fourteen. Maybe we'd had thoughts about it before that, but it was set in stone then. And that leads me to my next question. I have allowed and enjoyed someone other than a date or boyfriend to jack me off."

"Jesus, Bo. Just going to drop that out there, huh?" Kyson rammed a knee in the back of my seat.

"I don't *have* to give specifics, but for the benefit of our new friend, I will. When the three of us started hearing friends talking about girls' boobs and butts, we came to each other and kinda were like 'What the fuck? Why are they so interested in those girls?' A while later, Benji let it slip that he liked a Senior. When we finally got it out of him and he admitted it was Jimmy Medsker, Kyson and I admitted we'd been watching some of the guys in the locker room. One thing led to another and we all felt relieved to admit we liked guys. It was kinda nice coming out to each other first and having each other's support."

"What does that have to do with someone other than a date or boyfriend jack you off?" Sage frowned and stuck a chip in his mouth.

"Benji, Ky, and I were each other's *firsts* as far as hand jobs and blowjobs." I shrugged and Sage choked on his chip. "We never went further than that. But we'd grown up together since birth, Benji and I since conception, the three of us are closer to each other than to anyone else. When we realized we all liked guys, it made sense we'd experiment with each other to learn our way around being gay. At least at first." I braced myself for Sage's face to scrunch in disgust. Not a lot of people knew this information. I wasn't ashamed of it. There was nothing wrong with it. We were all consenting. We were the same age, none of us had power over the other. We weren't going to impregnate each other and mess up DNA. We learned what we liked with each other in a safe and comfortable environment.

Sage's face was pink, but he let go of the breath he'd been holding. "Fuck, that's so hot."

Kyson, Benji, and I all busted out laughing.

"Not gonna lie, yeah, it was pretty damn hot. Inexperienced, gangly, exploding way too quick, but hot."

Kyson reached around the seat and squeezed my shoulders. "I can't believe you just threw that at him."

I shrugged and glanced at Sage. "You're okay with it? Some people aren't."

"Do you guys still…" he paused and chewed on his lip, "hook up?"

"No. Haven't done that since we were horny teens experimenting. I'm not against people who do, but we've not found reason to do that with each other anymore." I opened a candy bar and took a bite. "Your turn to answer."

Sage's eyes went wide. "No, I've never allowed someone other than a date to jack me off."

"Or boyfriend?" Kyson nudged Sage's leg with his knee.

"Haven't really ever had a real boyfriend," Sage mumbled.

Holy fuck.

"But you've dated and messed around, right?" Benji asked. He wasn't judging, just making conversation. Not exactly *casual conversation*, but it didn't seem too probing.

"In for a penny, in for a pound," Sage murmured. "My grandma used to say that all the time. I guess since you spilled your guts, I can spill mine. Are all road trips like this?" He shook his head. "Anyway, yes, I've been on dates. I've messed around in that I've given and received one hand job and one blow job." He paused and looked directly at me. As if he was challenging me to grasp what he was saying. Like he expected me to make fun of him.

All of a sudden, what the kid was saying hit me like damn brick in the face.

I cleared my throat. "So, nothing beyond that?" *Oh my*

God. The kid was a virgin. When we'd pegged him as inexperienced, we hadn't known the half of it. *Holy shit.*

Sage nodded. "I've never really hit it off with the few dates I've been on. I don't think I'm one for random, pointless hookups. I'm not purposely holding out, just haven't found anyone who likes me well enough to have sex with."

"Anyone who doesn't like you well enough doesn't deserve to have sex with you." I bit out the words and turned in my seat to stare out the front with my arms folded across my chest. "Nothing wrong with being a virgin." I felt the need to assure him of that.

The game was over.

And just like that, there was another tally in the *Sage and Bode have no fucking reason to even consider being together* category.

The very last thing I needed was to be responsible for the sexual awakening and education of this beautiful boy.

Fuck.

6

SAGE

I WAS TORN between being embarrassed to admit my inexperience and my heart soaring over having three friends I felt pretty much comfortable enough with to tell them the truth.

While it wasn't *easy* to tell three men who were older than me and clearly much more experienced than me that I had next to zero sexual experience, I knew without a doubt that none of them would make fun of me or hold it against me. Even gruff and grumpy Bode. And I was right. While Bode didn't seem happy with the information, he definitely took a protective stance rather than judging me.

While I was a virgin, and I felt okay telling them that, it didn't feel like the right time to explain I wasn't clueless or uneducated in sexual acts, desires, and likes/dislikes. Maybe there would never be a reason to delve deeper into that. I gave a mental shrug and focused on what the guys were saying.

"If you ever want our help in meeting guys or advice about dating, anything like that, just let us know." Benji slapped me on the shoulder once we'd piled out of the car at the state park where we were going to hike before heading to their hometown.

"Yeah, we've got single friends. You could always bring a date to the Lizard as a safety net, let us check him out, be there as support if needed." Kyson propped his foot on a split-rail fence and tied his shoe.

"Kid doesn't need our dating advice. Not like any of us are actually *dating* anyone. And I'm pretty sure he doesn't want us playing matchmaker. Right, Sage?" Bode frowned with his arms folded over his chest.

I shrugged. "I don't have any prospects right now. And I'm pretty busy with school." I took a sip of water. "But I wouldn't mind you guys checking him out and giving me pointers if it ever gets to that."

Bode scowled and mumbled something unintelligible as he turned to stalk toward the path. Benji and Kyson both laughed and sent winks my way. I wondered at all three reactions, but I shrugged and caught up with them for our hike.

We spent the next ninety minutes traveling paths through a beautiful Indiana forest. Fall was right around the corner and the very tiniest inklings of the season change were starting to show on a leaf here and there. The day was warm, but there was a different feel to the air that let a native Hoosier know summer maybe hadn't given up completely just yet, but she was starting to lose her fight.

Fall was my favorite season. I loved watching summer come to an end. Loved the way the heat and humidity struggled to maintain its hold but slowly gave way to cooler and cooler air until there was an actual bite in the brisk breezes which blew through the magnificently colored leaves decorating our deciduous trees. Fall was always a new start to school too and this year was no different.

But it *was* different. Not only was I in a new year of schooling, I had new friends. Possibly the very first real friends I'd ever had.

Friends who had invited me on a road trip. Friends who shared secrets with me. Friends who didn't judge me for being me.

And one of those friends was trekking in front of me with the finest ass I'd ever seen in my life. Bode was grumpy and gruff. Bode was somewhat standoffish. He was fiery and determined. The life of the party. But Bode was also protective—recently of *me* it seemed. And Bode was drop dead gorgeous.

I ducked to avoid a branch slamming into my face and sighed. There was so much I could learn from Bode—despite the fact that he saw me as some nerd who knew it all. About owning a business, about being more outgoing...about *sex*. My groin clenched. I knew next to nothing about sex. Sure, I knew the mechanics and I'd been up close and personal with two cocks other than my own. And I'd done *a lot* of playing with sex toys. But my heart fluttered and my breath caught in my chest at the thought of all that Bode could show me.

But Bode Silver saw me as nothing but a kid. He wasn't interested in dating. He was head-over-heels involved with his business. Even if I thought I was the type to be okay with a casual hookup, would Bode ever be able to move past me being younger than him?

The four of us chatted and joked around as we made our way along the trail, stopping every so often for selfies and pictures with the gorgeous nature background. By the time we reached the car we were all ready to sit down. We each drained a bottle of water and wiped the sheen of sweat from our foreheads.

"Tick check!" Benji called. "I'll do Kyson. Bo, you do Sage. Then switch."

I knew what ticks were, of course. I'd lived in Indiana my whole life. But I wasn't familiar with a *tick check*. I caught Bode's murderous glare directed toward his brother, but I watched Benji in order to learn what I should do.

Benji ran his hands over Kyson's hair, checking thoroughly behind his ears. Then he ran his hands all over Kyson's shoulders and torso before skimming the waistband of his shorts. Finally, Benji moved his hands down Kyson's legs and ran fingers under Ky's socks.

"Very thorough." Kyson winked at his cousin and began his own check of Benji.

Bode frowned. "Come here." He stood with his legs apart. "Check me. They wouldn't likely be attached yet, but we want to get them off before they have time to suck on."

My cheeks heated as I ran my hands through Bode's hair and peeked behind his ears. I swallowed thickly and prayed my dick would behave as my hands traveled over his rock hard chest and torso; he wasn't huge, but he definitely had muscle definition. He reminded me of a basketball player or swimmer in that he was tall with lean muscle rather than beefy muscle. I glanced at Bode's stony face and my gaze darted away. I skimmed his waistband and moved toward his legs. His legs were solid under my touch and I sensed the strength in them. After peeling his socks away from his skin in one last check, I let out a breath I didn't even know I'd been holding.

"All good," I mumbled.

"Let's go, Bo. Check Sage so we can hit the road." Benji ordered and he and Kyson climbed in the car and sat with the doors open.

Oh my God. Bode was going to touch me. It wouldn't *mean* anything. But he'd still have his hands on me. If ever there was a time I needed my dick to be oblivious, it was that moment.

My eyes closed automatically as Bode's hands dug into my hair. He rubbed my scalp with his fingers and I forced back a groan. Damn, how did that feel so good? I laughed a little as he checked behind my ears. "I feel like monkeys eating insects off their partner."

Bode snorted.

His hands brushed my shoulders and roughly moved along my chest and torso. I couldn't help the squirm of my body as he reached my most ticklish spots. "Sorry, ticklish."

Bode clenched his jaw as his hands made quick work of moving over my waistband.

I immediately regretted the mental image assaulting my brain as he knelt to check my legs. His head was right at crotch level. If Bode ever gave me a blowjob on his knees, that was the view I'd get. My cock twitched. I tensed as his hands traveled down my legs. We both seemed to breathe easier once he'd checked my socks.

"You're good. Let's go." Bode pushed to his feet and stalked to the car.

Who knew checking for ticks would be such a turn-on?

* * *

We pulled onto a sprawling lane that dipped down a hill before ascending and breaking into a V. To the right was a large, renovated farmhouse. To the left was a nearly identical home.

"That's where Bode and I grew up." Benji pointed to the right.

"And that's mine." Kyson pointed to the left.

Benji took the fork in the lane leading to his childhood home. He parked the car along the side of a barn and we all climbed out. As I stretched my arms and legs, I took in the property.

Money was evident, but the house and other buildings were very understated. If I were to venture a guess, I'd figure most of the money was in the interior décor, well-invested stocks and bonds, and vehicles. From a quick scan, I determined the Silver family liked their cars, trucks, mowers, tractors, utility vehicles, and four-wheelers. All were parked in garages or sheds or shop bays, and all were in pristine condition. And there were *a lot* of them.

"Mom said we're all eating here." Kyson gestured over his shoulder. "I'll take my bag to my house after dinner."

"Time to meet the family." Benji rested his hands on my shoulders and jostled me. "Don't worry, they will likely be on their best behavior."

"Yeah, my dad doesn't like to dredge up our dirty laundry—otherwise known as *me*—in front of guests. It should be fairly comfortable." Bode rolled his eyes through his scowl.

I may have had pretty aloof parents who constantly

made me feel that no matter what I did I'd never live up to their ridiculous expectations, but the hurt and anger in Bode's words were like an arrow to my heart.

"You shouldn't have to feel that way," I mumbled and cast a quick glance toward Bode.

"It is what it is." He shrugged.

"You'll prove 'em wrong when The Salty Lizard is the most happen' place on Mass Ave." Kyson slapped Bode on the back.

"Or prove him right when it goes belly up." Bode's words were soft and he pursed his lips.

"Bo gets a little tense whenever we're home. Dad has always been harder on him than on me or Ky." Benji wrapped his arm around his brother as he explained things to me. "Dick and Rod Silver are rich and successful and very good at what they do. But they aren't exactly the most nurturing and supportive fathers in the world. They've always provided for us in all areas *except* emotional support."

"Maybe your dads and my parents should get together and compete over who can set the most ridiculous expectations or be the most disappointed in their kids' failures." I wrinkled my nose. I hadn't even met the men yet, but I already didn't like Dick and Rod Silver very much.

"At least our moms are pretty amazing. I think we all got our social emotional skills from them." Kyson swept his arm wide. "Shall we?"

Benji and Kyson led the way with Bode and I following.

Without a single thought as to what I was doing, I reached over and took Bode's hand and gave it a squeeze. "I know how much it sucks to constantly be under a microscope and judged wanting. If you need an out, feel free to give me a signal. I'll pretend to choke or something."

Bode nearly gave himself whiplash looking my way, but he squeezed my hand back and smiled. "Or maybe you could be a little less dramatic and just ask me to show you to the restroom?"

My cheeks heated and I chuckled. "I guess. If that's the route you want to take."

When Kyson turned to say something to us, Bode released my hand as if it was a snake. But definitely not before Kyson saw and his eyes grew wide. He turned back and said nothing.

Bode cleared his throat. "Thanks. I doubt Dad will be too much of an asshole. He always wants to impress guests. *'Never know when a stranger may become a potential client.'*" Bode made his voice deep.

"Your dad kinda sounds like a douche," I mumbled. "Sorry."

"No need to apologize. He is." Bode ruffled his hair. "You have no idea."

"Well, now I'm even more determined that you're going to make the Lizard amazing. He'll see how good you are." I gave a nod as if what I'd just said was truth just because the words came from my mouth.

Bode glanced down at me and smirked.

"What?" I wrinkled my brow.

He shook his head. "Nothing. Just not used to having a new member on Team Bode. It's kinda nice."

I smiled as we took the stairs to the house.

* * *

The Silver mothers, Janet and Debbie, were as kind and welcoming as could be. Rod, Kyson's dad, wasn't too terrible. I definitely liked him more than Bode and Benji's dad.

Dick Silver was just that. A dick. He smiled and said nice things, but everything he said felt fake. He was the epitome of a smarmy salesman. I guess being an insurance agent wasn't far from that.

Dinner was delicious and we all survived without me having to act like I was choking.

Janet and Debbie allowed the four of us to help clear the table while Dick and Rod each took a beer to the family room and flipped on the television. But the ladies shooed us from the kitchen when we offered to do the dishes.

"Gonna show Sage around the property," Bode called to whoever was listening.

Kyson, Benji, Bode, and I all traipsed outside.

"Hey, I'm going to sleep at Ky's tonight. We'll take our bags over and meet you back over here in a bit. Maybe four-wheelers and a bonfire?" Benji called these words over his shoulder as he walked toward his car.

"What?" Bode demanded. "Why?"

Benji shrugged. "Because I'm a nice guy and thought Sage would be more comfortable in my bed than on the couch or alone in the guest room." He lifted a hand. "You're welcome."

"He doesn't have to do that," I protested. "I can sleep wherever."

Bode's nostrils flared and he clenched his jaw. "No use arguing. Once he's decided something, there's no changing his mind."

"Did you guys ever own livestock?" I gestured toward the barn.

"We had pigs, sheep, cows, a few goats, and horses." Bode started toward the barn and I followed. "Never large numbers, just enough that we could show them in 4-H and win money when we placed high. Still have the horses, but our dads gave up the others when we weren't around as much to take care of the animals. Our moms like the horses and there's a farmhand who comes daily to care for them."

"Do your dads farm?"

"Nah, not them personally. We have plenty of acreage and they rent it out to local farmers. Most of our fields are used for corn and beans depending on the year." Bode opened the metal side door to the barn.

We stepped in and I was overcome with the sweet, earthy scent of hay, a packed dirt floor, and a smell that may have been oil. I breathed deeply. "Oh my gosh, it smells so good in here."

Bode smiled in the dim barn. "Doesn't it? I love the smell."

"Hay and dirt, I recognize. The other is familiar, like oil. Is that right?"

"Halfway. It's the oil used on the saddles. So, it's a mixture of oil and leather."

I took another deep breath and sighed. "God, I could live in here."

Bode chuckled. "The guys and I used to basically live here. We'd spend hours and hours playing in here. This has always been the horse barn. The bigger barn housed the cattle and pigs, the smaller one had the sheep and goats."

"There's a *bigger* barn?" I glanced around the expansive building. This barn was about the size of a quarter of a football field.

"Yeah, it's between the two houses. The guys and I convinced our dads to put a rope swing in the loft so we could swing from the loft and land on the hay." Bode pointed toward the hay loft. "Wanna try it?"

I laughed but then realized he was serious. "For real? Will it hold?"

"Guess we'll find out." Bode started up the wooden ladder. "Come on."

I stood rooted to my spot for several seconds while watching Bode's legs and ass as he climbed the ladder. Holy shit, that ass never ceased to take my breath away. I let go of the breath I was holding and started up the ladder behind him.

Bode reached for my hand and helped me into the loft. He unhooked the thick rope from its nail on the wall and gave it a hard yank. Dust motes burst from the rope and danced in the sunbeams streaming through the wooden planks of the barn walls. "Feels pretty sturdy."

I raised a brow. "You go first. I've never done this, I need to see what it entails."

Bode smiled and straddled the rope before sitting that perfect ass on the round wooden seat. "The seat is held up by a big ol' knot. It's not breaking loose. You just sit on it and jump off. You can swing for a while and then drop into the hay bales below."

It sounded terrifying and dangerous. My heart jumped into my throat when Bode launched himself from the loft and whooped loudly as he swung in a wide arc. After he swung back and forth a few times, he dropped gracefully on the hay.

"Your turn! I survived."

I bit my lip. "How do I get the rope back up here?"

"Oh, there should be a hooked stick up there. Stick it out and grab the rope."

I looked around the loft and found the stick. Once I had the rope pulled up to the loft, I straddled it the way I'd seen Bode do. If I let myself think about it for too long, I knew I'd climb down the ladder and not try the swing. I wanted to give it a shot.

"Okay, just jump!" Bode hollered up to me.

"Easy for you to say." I sat on the wooden seat and bounced a little to test it.

"Do it. I'll be down here to catch you if anything goes wrong." Bode stood in the hay piles with his hands on his hips looking fierce and protective, but smiling his characteristic grin.

With a deep breath, I closed my eyes and jumped. I screamed the entire way down, but it was a thrilling drop. I finally opened my eyes and enjoyed swinging for a few moments.

"Drop down here."

When I was near Bode, I let go of the rope and fell the rest of the way. When I landed, I lost my balance, arms flailing, and began to topple to the ground.

Strong arms grabbed me from behind and held tight until I stopped wobbling. Bode's mouth was at my ear, his front plastered to my back, his arms wrapped around me. "Whoa, gotcha. You okay?"

My heart switched from nearly pounding out of my chest to an almost dead stop. Bode's heat and strength warmed my body and had me fighting the urge to lean into his lips. I wanted so badly to tip my head back, to welcome Bode's mouth on my neck, to moan at his touch. Instead, I swallowed thickly and answered in a soft, husky voice. "Yeah, I'm good."

When it would have made sense for Bode to loosen his grip and step away, the man seemed to hold me tighter for a couple seconds more. I heard his gulp near my ear before he let out a breath and gently let go.

He moved away and stepped onto the dirt floor.

I followed.

We stood quietly for an awkward moment.

Bode cleared his throat. "Fun, right?"

I smiled and nodded. "Yeah, it was."

"That's why we spent so much time here."

"I can see why. So, what now?" I tried to act as if my heart wasn't about to beat out of my chest. As if I didn't want him to hold me close and kiss me.

Bode's jaw clenched and his nostrils flared almost as if he could read my mind. But that was ridiculous. He wouldn't ever go for someone like me. He'd made it clear I was just a kid and he had no interest.

"Let's go meet Ky and Benji. Get a fire going. You ever ridden a four-wheeler?"

When I rolled my eyes and smirked, he laughed.

"Okay, I'll take that as a no. I'll teach you."

We left the barn and headed toward a huge open area where I saw a gigantic pile of sticks and limbs. I'd heard tell of bonfires, but I'd never actually experienced one. I scanned the area around me as we walked. Four horses grazed in a pasture. Benji and Kyson headed toward us on four-wheelers. And Bode paused to grab a can of what I assumed was gasoline or similar as he mumbled something about needing a good starter fluid.

"What are you thinking about?" He bumped my shoulder.

"Just that we grew up *so* very different." I chuckled at the understatement.

"Proof that opposites attract," Bode quipped then froze. "I mean, opposites can be friends," he stumbled over his words.

"Yeah, I know what you mean." I smiled. I did know what he meant. I was so happy to have these new friends. But a tiny part of me mourned that moment in the barn as what would never be.

7

BODE

FUCK. What the hell was I doing?

Catching Sage in the barn should have just been me helping him. Not my lips at his ear, my body pressed to his, my cock taking an immediate interest.

And my damn brother offering his bed to Sage would have been an act of kindness if I didn't know better. Benji did that on purpose to put Sage and me together. Benji and I shared a room. So tonight, I'd be sharing a room with Sage.

Fuck.

And now I had to teach Sage how to drive a four-wheeler.

"Okay, I'll take you on a loop around the property. Then I'll ride behind you while you get the feel for it. Pretty soon all four of us will ride on our own." I tossed a helmet to Sage and climbed on the machine. "Get on."

Benji and Kyson had already taken off on their own vehicles, so I turned mine on and slid my helmet on. Dad had a client who had fallen from a recreational vehicle and suffered permanent damage so he'd instilled the use of helmets in us from the first time we were allowed to ride or drive.

"Just hold on to me. Get the feel of how it moves. Pay attention to the sound and feel when I shift gears." I put the four-wheeler into first gear and slowly began to move forward.

Sage was trying to keep his distance, but his arms immediately wrapped around my waist and he scooted closer so that his thighs encased my hips.

As we made our way around the property, Sage's grip on me loosened slightly. By the time we got back to our starting point, his green eyes sparkled under the helmet and his face was bright with a smile.

"That was great! I don't even need to learn to drive it, I'd have fun just riding."

I climbed from the vehicle. "Nah, it's even more fun to drive. Scoot up."

Sage slid up the seat to the driver's position and I climbed on behind him.

I spent a couple minutes showing him how to shift gears and then reached my arms around him and placed my hands on his. "Go ahead, shift into first gear. Give it some gas. We'll start slow and then I'll let go."

Within only a couple minutes, Sage had mastered driving the four-wheeler so I moved my hands from his and rested them lightly on his hips. As Sage drove us up and down hills, through the pasture, and along the winding path between the houses, I counted trees and birds trying to keep my mind from how easy it would be to slide my hands to the tops of Sage's legs. How easy it would be to rock my hips and press against him. My hands itched to travel from a light touch on his waist up his torso to skim along his chest.

Fuck. What the hell was wrong with me? He was a renter. An employee. And now a friend. My mind and body had no damn business showing an interest in the kid. *Kid* being the operative word as I recalled how innocent he was. Yes, he was well beyond the age of consent, but there were way too many reasons I shouldn't get involved.

If only my head and my dick would listen to those reasons.

* * *

We spent the next couple hours roasting hot dogs and marshmallows at the fire, enjoying a few beers, and shooting the shit like the old days.

"How many nights you think we spent out here?" Kyson tipped his head back, eyes on the wide expanse of stars above.

"I'd say we had one or two bonfires a week. Sometimes three or four during the summer. Maybe not full-sized bonfires, but at least campfires. Nothing beats hot dogs, beer, fire, and friends." Benji sighed and sipped his beer.

"Do you guys miss this? Being in the city and away from this?" Sage gestured around us.

"Sometimes. But we like the city as much as we like this. And we're close enough that we can come do this any time we want. And the city keeps us away from the porn brothers." I popped two more marshmallows on my stick.

Sage chuckled. "I can't believe you guys call your dads the porn brothers. Do they know?"

"Yeah, they hate it. Say we're being childish." I shrugged. "They're just mad their folks saddled them with such terrible names to go with the last name Silver."

About an hour later, the fire was burning itself out and Sage was yawning.

"Let's douse the fire and head to bed. Supposed to rain tomorrow. We could hang in the basement until it's time to go." Kyson turned on the water hose and sprayed the remaining embers.

The four of us packed up the food and gathered the trash.

"See ya in the morning for breakfast. I think Mom said she'd cook." Benji gave a wave.

Once Sage and I reached the house and quietly put away the food, I was about to bite through my tongue with awkward anticipation of sharing a room with Sage. Would he be upset about sharing the room?

We grabbed our bags from the front foyer and headed up the stairs.

"I feel bad that Benji gave me his bed. Which is his room?" Sage stood in the hallway looking at the doors.

"Don't feel bad, he'll be comfortable over at Ky's." I cleared my throat. "Mom and Dad's room is downstairs. That's a bathroom and a closet." I gestured toward the other doors. "Benji and I share a room."

Sage's eyes went wide, but he recovered quickly. "Oh, well that makes sense." He shrugged.

I opened the door to my bedroom.

And froze.

Holy shit. I knew Mom had remodeled the downstairs

guest room into her craft room, but I didn't realize she'd remodeled *our* room into a guest room. New hardwood floors, new paint, new color scheme, and a new king-sized bed.

One bed.

Where Sage and I were supposed to sleep.

I stood and stared at the bed for several beats before I finally snapped out of it. "Well, shit. Mom must have decided to remodel sooner than we thought. Um, I'll just sleep on the floor."

Sage snorted. "Don't be ridiculous. It's a hardwood floor. I can sleep on the couch."

"No, none of our couches are good for sleeping. They may be pretty, but they aren't super comfy." I wasn't going to make the kid sleep on the couch. Selfishly, I didn't want to cramp myself on our couches either.

"What about the basement? I can sleep there. I don't want to make things weird for you."

"The basement is stuffy. It's not that big of a deal. As long as you're not uncomfortable that is. It's a huge bed, it's not like we'd have to play spoons." I gestured toward the bed and cocked my brow at Sage.

He took a deep breath. "Yeah, you're right. I'm fine with it."

I sighed and tossed my bag in one of the armchairs. "At least it looks like a really nice bed. Should be comfy."

Sage smiled and followed my lead by dropping his bag on the other armchair. He glanced around the room. "So, this is where you slept as a kid?"

I frowned. "Yeah, but it's all different now. She took down all our stuff." I'd known Mom would eventually remodel, but it still kinda sucked to see our childhood room set up as an impersonal guest room. I cleared my throat. "Um, you can have this bathroom. I'll use the hall one." I showed Sage where the towels were located and left him to shower while I made my way to the hall bathroom.

When I got back to the bedroom, Sage was curled up under the blankets on the left side of the bed. I usually ended up on the left side, but it wasn't that big of a deal. I saw the neck of Sage's t-shirt and decided I'd put a shirt on. Did he have on pajama pants? I pulled a pair of basketball shorts on over my boxers and shrugged. I usually slept in just underwear, but I wasn't usually sharing a bed with a gorgeous, innocent friend. I'd deal with the extra layers.

I gingerly climbed onto the bed and slid under the covers. The bed was very large. I would have had to *try* in order to reach over and touch Sage. I took a few deep breaths. Okay, we could do this. It wasn't weird at all. The bed was comfortable. I was down home with my family and a new friend. I sighed contentedly into the pillow and settled in for a good night's sleep.

I woke to the smell of coffee and bacon on the air. I cuddled deeper under the comforter and held tight to the man in my bed.

My eyes shot open.

Fuck.

Somehow during the night, Sage and I had migrated from our own sides of the bed into the middle of the vast mattress. And I now played big spoon to Sage's little spoon.

I shut my eyes and gritted my teeth.

Holy fucking shit.

Sage shifted in my arms, his ass wiggling against my morning wood and his hand coming up to clutch at my arm across his chest.

He was soft and warm in my embrace. His hair smelled like last night's shampoo. And he wasn't awake enough to realize where he was just yet.

I should have launched myself from the bed before he woke and realized what was going on. But I was a selfish bastard and I couldn't bring myself to let go of him just yet. He felt so damn good.

And then he wriggled around and rolled over until we were facing each other. His hard cock was definitely awake. Sage nuzzled his nose against my chest and mumbled something that sounded suspiciously like my name.

Then, after one brief moment, I knew he was awake enough to know what was going on. He tensed and groaned.

I could feel our actual heartbeats in our throbbing cocks as they laid side-by-side through our pants. I tasted blood from biting my tongue and fighting the urge to thrust my dick against his.

Sage breathed deeply and his slowly released breath warmed my chest. "So much for a big bed, huh?"

I chuckled. "Yeah, um, sorry about that. I didn't mean for this to happen."

"Looks like I did my own amount of moving from my side." Sage started to stretch and then froze when the movement pressed our dicks together. "Oh shit, I'm so sorry." He hid his face in my chest.

"Don't sweat it. We're both in the same predicament." As much as I didn't *want* to move away from him, I knew I had to. Had to pretend like waking up with him in my arms hadn't been fucking amazing. It was a simple mistake. Didn't mean anything. I shifted my hips back and immediately missed the warmth of his body. Letting my arms loosen from around Sage's body, I scooted even farther away. "So, um, smells like breakfast is ready. I'm going to take a quick shower. You can go on down if you want, or wait for me. I'm sure Benji and Kyson are already here."

Sage nodded and rolled away from me. "Think I'll shower too."

We both stumbled toward our own bathrooms and spent the next fifteen minutes showering and dressing. I had a feeling that Sage and I both took advantage of the warm water to take care of our throbbing erections before slipping into casual clothing and running towels through our hair as if nothing awkward had happened.

I met Sage in the hallway and we headed downstairs for breakfast. We found my brother and Kyson in the kitchen. Our moms and dads had likely left earlier for church.

"Good morning!" Benji crowed much too brightly. "How'd you sleep?"

"Hey, Jee," I used the nickname I'd called my twin when we were toddlers, "did you know Mom remodeled our room?" I glared at him and poured myself a coffee.

"Oh really? New paint? I knew she was planning to change the room a bit." Benji chewed a piece of bacon.

I watched him closely. Had he known about the one bed?

"New hardwood floor, paint, color scheme. New king-sized bed." I didn't take my eyes from his as I spoke.

Benji's eyes grew wide and he bit his lip.

Kyson snorted.

I narrowed my eyes at them. "Yeah, so your act of kindness in sharing your bed with Sage kinda fizzled out when he had to share a bed with me."

Sage coughed. "No worries. It worked out fine." He shoved bacon in his mouth before mumbling, "Big bed, we fit. Not an issue."

My face heated as I recalled just how well *we fit* in each other's arms this morning.

Benji grinned like a damn fool and Kyson laughed out loud.

"Well, glad it all turned out okay. Could have been awkward." Kyson bit into a piece of toast.

"Yeah, could have been." I agreed and smeared peanut butter on my own piece of toast.

I glanced out the window. Rain came down in sheets. "We eating lunch here then heading back to Indy?"

Benji and Kyson nodded. "Let's hit the basement for some tournament play. After lunch we can hit the road."

The four of us cleaned up the kitchen before Benji and Ky headed down the stairs.

Sage caught my attention before we could catch up with them. "Hey."

When I looked at him his cheeks were pink.

"No harm, no foul this morning, okay? I know it didn't mean anything." He bit his lip.

"Yeah." I nodded. "Didn't mean anything." My jaw

ached from clenching it so hard. *Fuck*. If I wasn't careful, I would start believing that having Sage in my arms was a good idea and something I wanted to make happen.

I shook my head and followed him down the stairs. It may have been something I stupidly *wanted*, but it was most definitely *not* a good idea.

Twenty minutes later, I chuckled at Sage's frustration over his game of pool with Kyson.

Kyson smugly chalked his pool cue. "Sorry man, I'd give you some pointers but as your opponent, I don't think that's in my best interest."

"It's all about angles," Benji called from his place on the couch where he was playing a violent video game.

Sage lined up another shot and groaned loudly when he missed the pocket by a mile. "How can I suck at this so badly?"

I felt bad for the guy. Weren't the geeky guys supposed to have a knack for pool because they understood lines and angles and all that shit? Poor Sage was having a difficult enough time just holding his stick.

"Give him some pointers, Bo. I'm going to the bathroom and upstairs to get a drink. Rematch when I return." Kyson slapped Sage on the back.

After a couple minutes of telling and modeling how to hold the cue stick, I realized Sage wasn't getting it because he wasn't *feeling* it. I moved to stand behind him and positioned his arms and legs where they needed to be before handing him the stick and pressing my chest lightly against his back until he bent at his waist. I maneuvered his arms and hands until he was in the perfect position to take the shot. "Now, visualize the path you want the ball to take," I said softly against his ear.

The shiver that traveled through Sage electrified my body.

He took the shot and pressed his hips back against mine as he watched the cue ball strike the solid red three ball. He whooped when the ball dropped into a corner pocket. "Yes!" Sage pumped his fist. "Hurry, help me again. I've got to get better before Kyson gets back."

I laughed and followed him around the table while he decided on his next shot. He chose an easy one and looked over his shoulder expectantly. Who was I to deny the kid? I stepped close and posed him properly. "Picture where you want it to go." Even to my own ears my voice was gruff and low.

By the time Sage took and sank his third shot, I needed a drink and a breather. "I think you've got the hang of it. Just needed to feel it and get some good practice shots." I took the steps two at a time to escape the basement. I grabbed a beer from the fridge. Knowing Benji was driving meant I could drink without worrying about getting home. I took a long swallow from the bottle and leaned my arms against the sink while I looked out the window and sighed.

"Day drinking? That's the first sign of a problem." Benji hopped up on the kitchen island and grinned.

"Shut up." I took another swig of beer and spun around to face him.

"Damn man, you've got it *bad*. Why don't you just admit you like him and kiss him? I've seen the way his eyes undress you, pretty sure he'd be all for it." Benji's eyes flashed.

I gritted my teeth and tried to *not* imagine kissing

Sage. "It's not that simple. I've told you and Kyson about a thousand times why Sage and I wouldn't work."

"I apologize about the bed." Benji winced. "I thought sticking you two in the same room would make for some cute awkwardness. I didn't know Mom had switched to just one bed."

My face heated.

Benji's eyes grew wide. "Did something happen?"

I took a drink and stayed silent.

Benji stared at me.

"Fine," I snapped. I'd never been able to resist my brother's questioning. "We started on our own sides, but woke up all cuddled together."

Benji smirked. "And?"

I drained the rest of the beer. "And it was hot as fuck, okay?" I glanced toward the basement door. "But it can't happen. I'm not his type."

"And what exactly do you think is his type?" Benji raised a brow.

"Younger. Not his employer. Not his landlord. That's his type."

Benji shook his head. "Whatever you say, Bo." He slid off the island and pursed his lips. "So, you won't have any issues with Kyson and I getting Sage set up on a dating app? Try to get him some dates?"

My teeth were going to be damn nubs soon. My nostrils flared and I swallowed thickly. "Just make sure the guys aren't creeps. Make sure they're worthy of a date with him." My heart hurt. Sage deserved the best. I definitely wasn't the best. God how I wished I was. But none of that made it easier to think of Sage going out on dates.

Benji gave me a knowing look and a sad smile. "Sure thing, brother."

Three hours later, after a delicious lunch and thirty minutes of Dick Silver drilling me about The Salty Lizard and *his* expectations for how his money was to be used, *his* expectations on what he would deem successful, and *his* expectations as to what he wanted to see if and when he ever dropped by to visit, it was time to head home. What had been a relaxing, perfect weekend all of a sudden had me feeling pressure and stress. My head hurt after talking to my dad. My heart hurt thinking of Sage finding love.

Fuck. Adulting sucked.

8
———

SAGE

"WHAT'S HE DOING HERE?" Bode demanded in a harsh whisper a few days later as he stalked into the kitchen.

Without looking up from the napkins and plates I was gathering, I shrugged. "Bay brought Arlo over to play with me. We figured it was best to get to know each other here first and then I'll go visit Arlo and play. By then, we should be friends and Bay can have me watch Arlo as needed."

"You think you'll actually have time to babysit between school, studying, and the bar?" Bode crossed his arms over his chest.

I nodded. "Sure. He won't need me that often and I can take my studying over there. Arlo doesn't stay up late, so I can study after his bedtime."

"And when Bay gets home?"

I frowned. "I'll come home?"

"What if Bay makes a move on you?" Bode arched a brow.

I snorted. "Um, couple issues with that. First, pretty

sure Kyson would have my head. Second, Bay doesn't even glance my way because he's so busy with Arlo and ogling Ky. Third, if you think *you're* too old for me, what does that make Bay? He's more than twenty years older than me." I lifted my chin and didn't look away from Bode's hard gaze. "I'm not against being with an older guy, but Bay isn't interested in me any more than I'm interested in him."

Bode huffed and started searching the fridge.

"We've got pizza if you're hungry." I gestured toward the living room where Bay and Arlo sat on the floor playing with a building set the little boy had brought over. Bay's smirk told me he'd heard the entire conversation between Bode and me.

Bode shook his head. "Nah, I've got work to do." He walked to the living room and knelt by Arlo. "Hey, buddy, cool building." He gave the little boy a fist bump, directed a curt nod toward Bay, and retreated out the door. The fact that Bode was always kind and friendly to Arlo proved he wasn't nearly the grumpy ass he seemed to want me to believe.

Within moments, music blasted from the bar below as if Bode was attempting to drown out the fact that Bay and Arlo were in our living room. Or at least trying to forget the fact that *Bay* was in our living room.

Arlo, Bay, and I spent the next hour building with the blocks, knocking down our towers, eating pizza, playing bears and monsters, and laughing. Arlo was a great kid and we seemed to get along well.

Arlo climbed up on the couch next to me to watch one episode of a cartoon I'd never seen before. Within minutes, the little boy had curled up on his side and propped his head on my lap. My heart melted. Having kids wasn't something I'd spent a lot of time thinking about. I assumed that I'd give it more serious contemplation *someday*. After I graduated and found a partner and settled down. But having Arlo sleeping on my lap warmed something deep inside.

"He likes you." Bay smiled softly.

"He's a great kid. You're both lucky to have each other." I glanced down at the sleeping child.

Bay frowned for a brief second and then chuckled. "Yeah, Arlo is great and he likes you. But I was talking about Bode."

My eyes grew wide and my cheeks warmed. "Nah, I'm barely more than a nuisance to him." I meant the words, but my head thought back to our road trip, Bode giving me pool tips, swinging from the loft, and waking up in his arms. "He's glad to have my rent payment and a pair of extra hands in the bar. That's about it." Despite whatever all of that between us a few days ago had been, Bode continually made it clear that we weren't meant for each other.

"I get that you may not have a ton of experience with guys, but you'd have to be completely daft and blind to not see how bad that man has it for you." A smile played on Bay's lips. "He may hate it, he may be loath to admit it, but he likes you."

I started to protest, but stopped. "You really think so?"

Bay nodded. "How do you feel about him?"

My heart thumped and I knew a goofy grin teased at my lips.

"Well, that blush is as good an answer as any." Bay

stood and collected a sleeping Arlo from the couch. "You going to do anything about it?"

I stood and followed Bay to the door as I thought about his words. Finally, I ran a hand over my face. "Not sure there's really anything I *can* do. He's dead set against it. I'm busy with school. I have next to zero experience with dating or the like; I have *less* than zero experience with seduction. Plus, I wouldn't want to make things awkward. I need this place to live. The extra cash coming in from the bar is helpful. And I'd feel bad if I coerced him into something he didn't want."

Bay hefted Arlo in his arms and laughed softly. "Oh, he wants. He may not *want* to want. But he wants. Just keep being you. I have a feeling you two will eventually figure things out."

I shook my head. "There is no *you two*. He's a friend, a boss, and a roommate/landlord. Also, Benji and Kyson are going to set me up on a dating app. That could be fun, right?" Or it could be the worst thing ever.

Bay barked out a laugh loud enough that Arlo stirred. "Fun. Right. Let me know how that goes. I'm sure Bode will be a barrel of warm fuzzies when he has to think about you going out with other guys. Hell, he wants to pound my face in because I want you to watch my kid. Keep me updated." Bay chuckled softly and headed out the door.

* * *

"Let's get a good picture for your profile." Kyson grabbed my phone. "Stand in the kitchen, it's got good lighting."

I rolled my eyes, but went to the kitchen and let Kyson

order me around while he snapped several pictures. By the time we returned to the living room, Bode had poured another bowl of cereal and was angrily shoving spoonfuls into his mouth.

"What's got you so scowly?" Benji kicked at his brother's foot.

"Nothing. Just stressed about the opening."

Bode had a soft opening planned for Thursday with the grand opening happening Friday through the weekend.

Bode huffed and puffed, curled his lip and frowned, scoffed and rolled his eyes throughout the entire hour that Benji and Kyson helped me set up my dating app profile and scroll through the features. When my phone dinged with my first match, Benji and Kyson whooped and slapped me on the back.

Bode slammed his empty bowl onto the coffee table and left the room.

* * *

I tossed the notebook on my bed and groaned. I had a test the next day. I was supposed to head down to help in the bar in less than two hours, but I'd been reading the same damn notes for thirty minutes. Usually I was good at blocking out distractions and excess noise, but the excitement of The Salty Lizard's opening, mixed with the thumping music and my anxiety over a pretty huge test, had me flustered and unfocused.

Determined to study for at least another hour, I slipped on noise canceling headphones and cranked up my favorite instrumental study music in hopes of drowning out the bar and my own thoughts.

An hour later, I gave up and determined that if I didn't know the material by now I simply wasn't going to know it. I packed away my study materials and checked the time. I had time for a shower. The soft opening of The Salty Lizard had been at seven o'clock and it was now nine. I'd promised I could help until at least eleven. My class wasn't until later in the morning so I could probably stay until the midnight closing time.

I jumped in the shower, washed quickly, dried even quicker, and pulled on some of my *clubbiest* clothes. By the time I rushed down the stairs, I was pumped to help with the opening in any way Bode and the guys needed.

I went to the backdoor of the bar because I knew the storage room was cleared out since I was the one who did the cleaning. Bode jumped about a mile when I walked in; I clearly caught him off-guard.

"What the fuck, Sage?" Bode held a hand to his chest. "What are you doing here?"

I raised a brow. "Sorry, didn't mean to surprise you. I came down early."

"You're supposed to be studying." Bode's accusation was accompanied by a scowl.

I shrugged. "I was distracted. Thought I could help. I'm only like an hour early. How's it going? Sounds like a lot of fun is being had."

Bode ignored my question. "Opening night and you're already distracted? Great." He tossed his hands in the air. "So much for you being able to stay focused."

I bristled. "I'm a grown man, Bode. If I decide to stop studying a little early I'm perfectly capable of making that decision. It's *my* test, *my* grade."

"I won't be the reason you fail and drop out." He ran a hand over his face.

With a frown, I crossed my arms over my chest. "I'm top of my class, always have been. I'm in graduate school; I'm not some young first year student who doesn't know how to balance personal life and academic life. Back off." I realized Bode was stressed over his dad and the bar, but I wasn't going to stand there and let him berate me and act as if he was responsible for my schooling.

"I'm just saying, you *knew* the apartment was above a bar. You *knew* there'd be loud music and late nights. If you're thinking it was a mistake, say the word so we can find a replacement."

I flinched as if I'd been slapped. "You want me to move out?" My chest hurt.

"Of course not. I'm giving you an out. If it's all too much," he paused as if he didn't know how to finish what he was saying.

"Too much? The music and late nights? Or your messy ass leaving damn cereal bowls and milk cups all over the apartment? How about your grumpy ass constantly grumbling about anything and everything?" I stepped toward him with each word until we were so close we were almost touching.

Bode's nostrils flared with quick breaths. "Oh, are we getting personal now? Have you ever heard of sleeping in? How about you vacuum at a time that's *not* the ass crack of dawn? Do you *have* to do dishes first thing in the morning? You sound like you're purposely clanging the damn glasses together just trying to make the most noise possible."

I scoffed. "That's rich! Maybe if you didn't leave your

mess everywhere, I wouldn't have to clean at all let alone at an early hour."

"You're a fucking genius, you could have found a quaint, quiet place with neat and tidy smart guys instead of slumming it with us!" Bode wasn't yelling, but his whisper was harsh.

I pressed my hand against his chest until his back hit the shelving unit. "You're right, I *am* smart. Which means I'm damn smart enough to know where the hell I want to live. I didn't *have* to live with the three of you. I chose you and felt lucky when you picked me. Yeah, the music is loud and the bar is open late, but have some fucking faith and confidence in me to know I'm a big boy and can make my own damn decisions. I was distracted tonight mostly because I was excited to come down here and help *you* with this bar. It's *your* dream, but I want to be part of making it come true." When I finished my tirade, I was breathing heavily with my hand still on Bode's chest.

Before I could drop my hand, he spun me around so my back was against the shelves. "You're fucking hot as hell when you're all worked up." His words were a growly whisper and his breath was hot against my ear.

Oh, shit.

"Um, what?" I didn't know how to respond. One moment we were arguing and the next moment he had me pressed against a metal rack of bar supplies telling me I was hot as hell when I yelled at him. My head spun. And my dick was totally on board with Bode's body being so close.

"Jesus." Bode's voice cracked as he backed away from me and ran a hand through his hair. "I'm sorry, that was *not* appropriate at all. I'm a fucking mess trying to make this bar a success to prove myself to my dad and I'm taking it out on you. I'm sorry."

At that moment, Kyson popped his head around the corner. His eyes grew wide as he glanced between Bode and me. "Sorry to interrupt, but you've got some customers wanting to meet you, Bo."

"Not interrupting anything." Bode took another step away from me. "Be right out."

Kyson gave a nod with a smirk and left.

"Really, I *am* sorry. I shouldn't have griped at you and I most definitely should have *never* put you in that position. I was out of line."

I cocked my head and studied him. Right as Bode began to turn away from me, I gripped his arm. "We were both stressed and taking it out on each other. I'm sorry for yelling. But the rest of it? It didn't feel inappropriate. Not to me. Not at all." I swallowed thickly and bit my lip before forcing my eyes to look directly into his.

Bode glanced at where my hand held his arm and cleared his throat. "So, yeah. Um, I need to get out there. You want to straighten up anything you find back here and then come up front to help?"

"As long as I'm not drying glasses, I'll be glad to help." I smiled.

Bode chuckled and turned to leave despite my hand still keeping us connected.

"Bode?"

He paused to look at me.

"I was serious about wanting to be part of making the Lizard a success. I can't wait to see your dad eat his words and have to admit that you've done exactly what you set out to do. He'll see; everyone will see. You've got this." I squeezed his arm and let him go.

Bode's brow wrinkled. "Thanks."

"Is it really that hard to believe?"

Bode shook his head. "Sometimes I have my doubts. But it's not that. It's just very new to have anyone other than Benji or Kyson or our moms believing in me. New," he smiled, "but really nice. Thanks." He left me in the storage room.

My head and heart were going a mile a minute.

What the hell had just happened?

Did it mean anything?

I wanted it to mean something.

But would Bode want that?

Or was it just a tense and emotional situation leading to a mistake?

I scrubbed a hand over my face and set to work straightening the back room before building up the courage to go up front.

* * *

Thirty minutes later, the back room was immaculate and there wasn't a single item out of place or unaccounted for. My excuses were gone.

I moved to the front and stepped behind the bar. Kyson and Benji had donned bar aprons with The Salty Lizard logo so I grabbed one for myself. "How can I help?"

Benji, standing behind me, put his hands on my shoulders and jostled me. "Come meet some people first."

"No, that's not necessary. I can pour shots or pull drafts

or grab beers while you guys mingle." I wasn't confident in my ability to mix drinks just yet, but the rest I could totally handle. Bode had made sure I could do shots, drafts, cans, and bottles along with running the register, putting in food orders, and even preparing most of the food items. He hadn't had time yet to school me on mixed drinks.

"Nope, Bode wants you to meet everyone. Says the four of us are *the faces* of the Lizard." Benji gripped my elbow and pulled me toward several groups of people while my heart flip-flopped over Bode's words.

The four of us? Faces of the Lizard?

No way.

I understood Bode, Benji, and Kyson being the faces of the bar. But me? I was just hired help, the renter, the friend.

Bode clapped me on the back. "Here he is." He spoke to a group of four men and two women. "This is our friend, Sage. He's our roommate and helping around here when he's not busy being a genius and earning like ten degrees."

My face heated and I was glad the bar was mostly dim. My thoughts went back to the few moments we spent together in the storage room. The man was giving me whiplash. He didn't like me, he liked me, I was too young, I was hot, I was a nerd, I was a genius. He needed to make up his mind. But what if he made up his mind and ended up at not liking me at all? I rather liked what we had going on right then. Just wished it wouldn't be so confusing.

"Sage, these are some friends we've made since moving up here. Kurt, Chris, Mike, Matt, Jill, and Kathy.

Most of them work or live here on Mass. Ave." Bode pointed toward each person as he named them.

I smiled and said hello before Bode swept Benji, Kyson, and me toward another group.

After being introduced to three more groups of people, I noticed some people heading toward the bar. "I'll go grab their drinks." I broke from the group and hurried to get orders filled. Meeting so many people all at once and having Bode introduce me like I had been a part of their group for a long time had given me a thrill but was also overwhelming.

The bar began to clear out and I set to work wiping down empty tables, filling napkin dispensers, moving up product to the front counter and restocking the shelves. All too soon, the place was nearly empty and Bode walked the last customers toward the door.

Kyson cranked the music as Bode came back into the main part of the bar and Benji whooped as he jumped on his brother's back. I couldn't help the smile that spread across my face as Bode hung his head and held it in his hands. It was as if I could see the relief sagging on him.

Kyson grabbed me and pulled me along with him and we joined the group hug.

"You did it, Bo!" Benji wrestled with Bode before jumping off his back and hugging him close.

Bode nodded. "It was a good night, yeah?"

"So good. For a soft opening, it was amazing. This weekend should be packed. We've got the drink and food specials, the hype, the music, everything is in place. You're going to rock it just like we all knew you would." Kyson kept us all in a huddle and jumped us up and down.

"Celebration shots!" Benji shot his fist into the air.

We bellied up to the bar and Benji rushed behind the counter to fill eight shot glasses.

"To The Salty Lizard!" Kyson toasted and we all clinked glasses before swallowing the burning liquid.

Benji nudged the second shot toward me and gave me a nod.

My heart beat a thousand miles a minute, but I held up the glass and toasted. "To Bode and his dreams coming true."

Bode's eyes caught mine and held tight as we tossed back the second shot.

The fire in my belly and looseness in my limbs was just setting in when the song changed to "Bad Guy" by Billie Eilish.

Kyson grabbed me and pulled me to the dance floor.

"I'm not a good dancer," I protested.

But soon Benji and Bode joined us and I was just buzzed and hyped up enough to give in and start dancing. Kyson gripped my hips and pulled me flush to him with a laugh. I threw my head back and cackled; the move was laced with sexual intent, but nothing between Ky and I sparked sexually at all. We bumped together and swiveled our hips to the thumping rhythm blasting through the bar. Bode and Benji laughed and joined in—Bode behind Kyson, Benji behind me. We spent the rest of the song thrusting hips, grinding hips and asses, our arms thrown in the air.

When the song faded and was replaced by "Please Me" by Cardi B. and Bruno Mars, Benji spun me around just as Kyson moved and I ended up with my back plastered against Bode's front and Benji pressed against me with Kyson behind him.

The slower beat of the song caused us to transition from the bumping, thrusting, and arms up to a slow grind and arms wrapped around bodies. Benji's gorgeous face was in front of me as his body rocked against mine, but it was the heat of Bode's body plastered to my back that had my head spinning. When Benji reached for his brother's hips and pulled him close, there was no doubt that Bode was enjoying himself. I may have had very little experience, but that was definitely a rock hard cock against my ass.

Before my own dick betrayed me to Benji, I spun around to press myself against Bode. But the new position was no better. His hard length met mine and I instinctively pulled back, but we were magically sandwiched between Kyson and Benji and their rolling hips kept Bode and I flush together.

The music changed again and I dropped my buzzed head back on Benji's shoulder. My heavy eyes never left Bode's as Kyson pulled my hands up to Bode's shoulders. When Benji's lips skimmed my jaw and nuzzled against my neck, my knees nearly buckled. Not from Benji's touch, but from the fiery desire lighting Bode's eyes and the hard press of his thick cock against mine. Benji's lips on my skin felt good, but my heart hammered with desire wishing it was Bode's mouth on my neck.

The four of us rocked and swayed together until the song ended. We were left in an eerily silent bar in an intimate and awkward position.

I cleared my throat. "Congrats on a great opening, Bo. I really need to head to bed. Test tomorrow and all that." I ducked from the embrace and rushed toward the door.

I ran upstairs, showered, jacked off with images of

Bode playing through my mind, and climbed into bed before my roommates were even done downstairs. The evening had been strange, wonderful, and exciting. But the awkward tension had taken over there at the end and I had run away in an abrupt end to our time together.

By the time I heard the door open, I was nearly asleep.

Footsteps sounded outside of my room and stopped.

Bode?

Why was he standing outside my door?

"Sage, you awake?" Bode spoke quietly on the other side of the door.

I froze.

I wanted to answer. Invite him in.

But would he just offer more apologies and insist anything between us was a mistake?

I couldn't deal with that, not right then. I needed to sleep and do well on my test.

I kept my mouth shut and held my breath until Bode walked away.

When he turned on the shower, I rolled to my side intending to sleep.

The low moans I heard coming from our shared bathroom several moments later did absolutely *nothing* to help me fall asleep.

9

BODE

HOLY.

Fucking.

Shit.

I watched Sage rush from the bar.

What the hell was happening? And what the hell was wrong with me?

The evening had started with nerves and stress, but I had high hopes the soft opening would go well. When Sage burst in the back door, I let my nerves get the best of me and I snapped at him.

I felt bad about jumping all over him. He was smart and grown, he could decide to stop studying. I shouldn't have reacted the way I did.

But holy mother of God, I *really* shouldn't have let myself somehow end up so close to him that I could whisper in his ear how damn hot he was.

I ran a hand over my face and stalked to the restroom. I needed to get control of my damn cock and calm down.

By the time I no longer sported a traitorous bulge, I found my brother and cousin finishing the last of the cleanup. "What the hell do you two think you're doing?"

The fuckers had the audacity to look at me with blank, innocent faces.

"Stop pushing Sage on me." I threw an arm toward the ceiling as if pointing to Sage. "And stop pushing me on him. We aren't a match. There's too much difference between us. We've had this conversation. Knock it off." I crossed my arms over my chest.

"Just having some fun with friends. If you're feeling something towards Sage, that's your deal." Benji shrugged and turned off the lights behind the bar.

"I don't know, Bo. You keep protesting, but I see the way you two look at each other. I saw whatever the hell that was in the back room. I saw how you looked like you wanted to devour him on the dance floor. Maybe you're pushing away something amazing." Kyson placed a hand on my shoulder.

I took a deep breath and prayed for patience. "I've never said the kid wasn't attractive. Of course, I'm going to react to him when you two have us sandwiched together in a bump and grind. But that doesn't change the fact that he's too young, he's a renter, and he works for us. It's too much."

Benji and Kyson stared at me for a moment and then shrugged.

We tramped up the stairs. Benji and Kyson immediately retreated to their rooms.

I headed toward mine, but I was drawn to Sage's door like a magnet. I should apologize for all the inappropriateness of the night. I should make sure he understood there couldn't be anything between us.

Or do you just want to see him? Have an excuse to be in his room, close to him?

I knocked softly. "Sage, you awake?"

When I got no answer, I went to my room and stripped off my clothes. I needed a shower and sleep. I had a grand opening to prepare for.

Walking into the bathroom I shared with Sage, I was assaulted with the scent of his soap and shampoo. My dick immediately hardened and I groaned. I turned on the water, climbed into the stall, and vigorously washed my hair in hopes of losing my erection. But I was surrounded by the lingering smell of his shampoo and I stupidly picked up his bar of soap and took a long whiff.

Fuck.

Without a second thought, I soaped my hand and gripped my cock. Sage was the star of my fantasy and I didn't even try to control my moans as I came.

* * *

The next morning, I grumbled into my pillow as I heard the damn vacuum outside my door. Rolling from bed, I took a piss, washed my face, and pulled on some pants.

Sage was finishing at the end of the hallway and switched off the sweeper.

"Good morning, my little vacuuming fiend. How was your test?"

He jumped and I chuckled.

"Sorry, but there were grass clippings. I think we must have tracked them in last night after taking the trash out back. Test went well." Sage went to the kitchen and poured a glass of juice. He held up the carton for me. Okay, so maybe we were acting as if last night didn't happen.

I nodded and he poured a glass for me.

"Can I ask you a question?" He stared at me over the rim of his glass.

Oh hell. Here we go. I nodded. "Sure."

"Why did you introduce me as one of *the faces* of the Lizard?"

Oh. That wasn't what I was expecting.

I frowned. "Why not?"

"Because I'm not family."

"You may not be blood family, but I consider you more part of the bar than my father. You're one of us. You work there. You're part of what will make the Lizard special." I swallowed the rest of the juice. "Benji and Kyson are there a lot *now*, but they'll be focused on their own businesses soon enough. I know you can't be there full-time, but I think of you as one of the founding members. You're the first real employee I hired. Sure, I've got others coming on, but the four of us are the originals." I stared at my empty glass for a moment. "I guess I can't really even explain it. You just fit with us and I think of you as one of us and part of the Lizard."

Sage shook his head. "I've never in my life had anyone consider me part of anything. My grandma loved me. Mrs. Phegley cared about me. But no one has ever included me in something as big as this." His words were quiet and I wasn't sure if he was talking to me or himself.

"Well, there's a first time for everything." I put my

glass in the sink. "Hey, about last night," I started but stopped when Sage held up a hand.

"No worries. Just the excitement and stress and didn't mean anything. No harm, no foul." Sage rinsed his own cup and then did the same to mine while glaring at me. "See how easy that was? A quick rinse means fewer dishes later."

I rolled my eyes.

He grumbled.

I ignored him and rubbed my hands together. "You want to learn those mixed drinks today?"

Sage smiled.

My chest tightened.

Fuck. I *had* to get this shit under control.

"Let's go." I stalked from the kitchen and down the back steps.

* * *

"Are you purposely trying to be an ass?" Sage blew a strand of hair from his forehead and put his hands on his hips. He was helping me finalize inventory in the back room.

Was I? No, not purposely. But I wanted the grand opening to be perfect. That meant making sure everything was just right.

"Sorry, I just want it all to go exactly as planned." I took a deep breath and blew it out of puffed cheeks.

"Nothing ever goes as planned." Sage's words were quiet as his stance softened slightly. "You are ready and prepared. Your plans are backed up and your back-ups have back-ups. But none of that will guarantee the opening goes as planned."

I sighed. "I know, you're right."

"Yep." Sage smiled and winked.

I rolled my eyes and chuckled. "Sorry, I just keep hearing my dad's words and seeing his disapproving face in my head and I'm freaking out a bit."

"It's okay." Sage stepped closer and put his hand on my shoulder. "The soft opening was amazing and I think the big one will be even better. The guys and I will be here for you. Try not to let your dad's negativity and low expectations invade your mind. Keep it positive, keep it light, think of your friends and customers and how the Lizard is your dream come true."

The warmth of his hand, the scent of his skin, the closeness of his body all had my senses on overload. I clenched my jaw and swallowed hard. If Sage noticed my reaction to his proximity he likely assumed it was in response to the talk of my father.

"Let's go make those drinks. I have a feeling I'm going to need a lot of practice." Sage gestured toward the front of the bar. "Good thing I know you have plenty of supplies in stock for all my mess-ups."

I laughed. "Boy, you're not wasting my ingredients. You'll learn them and do them right within a couple tries or mixed drinks go the way of wiping down glasses."

Sage's eyes went wide. "Pretty soon, there will be nothing for me to actually do in the bar. I'll be resigned to hide in the back room with only the toilet paper as company."

I snorted. "Come on."

An hour later, Sage groaned. "Oh my God. You can't be

serious. That tastes perfect. You're going to make me do it again?"

"Only because it *is* perfect and I want a full one." I slapped him on the back. Sage had proven to be an excellent student and picked up mixology quicker than I could have ever hoped for.

He laughed after he nailed each drink recipe after recipe. "There's a lot of science in recipes and mixing. Maybe that's why it comes easy for me." He held up the color-printed packet of laminated and illustrated drink recipes. "And having this is a lifesaver."

"Those are the top twenty drinks. I'm sure you'll get requests you're not sure about. You can ask the person or look it up on your phone. You're so good at the proper ratios, I'm sure you'll learn the unknown drinks quickly and probably even come up with your own concoctions."

Sage beamed at the simple praise and my heart clenched. This kid deserved to hear how wonderful he was every single day. *You could be the one telling him that.* I tried to push away the thought, but Sage spoke and my heart flip-flopped.

"Thanks. I know it's ridiculous, but it's nice to be told I'm good at something. No matter how well I did in school, my parents always expected more and better." Sage dipped his head and turned away from me—out of embarrassment? Because he felt emotional?—to wipe down the already spotless counter.

I moved closer so I could hear his quiet words. *And because you like to be close to him.*

"I know it's just stupid mixed drinks, but it makes me feel good to know I'm good at something outside of school." Sage turned around unexpectedly. "Ya know?"

With his back to the bar, his surprised and vulnerable face so near mine, I felt Sage's breath as he voiced his question. Without a second to think through my next move, I nudged his chin with a finger and lifted his face until he was staring into my eyes. I dipped my head and brushed my lips over his.

My head and heart screamed in silent disagreement. My heart rejoiced and demanded I deepen the kiss, pull Sage into my arms, own him. My head argued that a soft brush of my lips on his was already enough of an overstep and I needed to pull back, retreat, protect him and myself.

The battle was ended when Sage whimpered and reached up to wrap his arms around my neck. His mouth opened and all sense left me as my lips and tongue accepted his invitation. We kissed for several moments, simply enjoying the closeness, until the back door slammed and we broke apart so quickly my head and body both shuddered from the loss of contact.

Sage touched fingers to his kiss-swollen lips and his cheeks reddened. "I'm so sorry, I shouldn't have done that."

I wanted to pull him into my arms and reassure him, but voices came down the hall. "No, don't apologize. I was the one who started it. I'm sorry."

Sage smiled softly with his fingers still resting on those damn gorgeous lips.

"But you've got to know," I began.

His smile turned sad. "I know. Means nothing. Just the stress and nerves. I get it." Sage turned and cleaned up the mess from our Drink Mixing 101 class just as Kyson and Benji came around the corner.

The four of us spent the next hour talking and

laughing and sampling Sage's amazing mixed drinks. Sage acted as if nothing had happened. Should I take his cue and do the same? If I admitted that *something* had happened between us, I'd have to admit to wanting it, liking it, hoping it happened again. Was that a road I was prepared to take?

I swallowed thickly. No. I needed to be mentally, physically, and emotionally prepared to devote my time and energy to The Salty Lizard. Period.

Later that night, we celebrated a grand opening that was more successful than my wildest imagination allowed me to hope for. When the last customer left at one in the morning, Kyson, Benji, Sage, and I piled into a huge hug and whooped our excitement. By 2 a.m., the bar was cleaned and locked up as we made our way upstairs. The smile refused to leave my face.

I was still beaming and replaying the night in my room when the bathroom door creaked open. Sage stood in his sleep shorts and shirt with wet hair and steam billowing behind him.

"I wanted to tell you again. Congratulations on such an amazing night. And thank you for letting me be a part of it." He stepped closer and threw his arms around me. "I never thought I'd have friends and belong like I do here. Thank you."

I tensed for a brief moment before relaxing into the hug. "I wouldn't have it any other way. Didn't realize we had room for a fourth in our little posse, but now I can't imagine not having you here." My words were one-hundred percent the truth.

Sage pulled away from the hug with a happy smile on his face and a tear in his eye. "Good night."

Swallowing thickly, telling myself it would be a mistake to yank him back into my arms, I winked. "Good night."

Sage went back to his room and I spent the rest of the night trying to convince myself that I wasn't the right guy for him. That we were too different. But the touch of his lips and the taste of his tongue lingered and provided a convincing argument against all of my protests.

10

SAGE

A FEW DAYS after the kiss I was desperately trying not to fantasize about, I had a classmate over for a study session. I introduced Bruce to the guys and then we disappeared into my room for two hours of studying and working on a project.

When we emerged, I was grumpy, hungry, and tired. I saw Bruce quickly to the door and curtly told him I'd see him in class.

"Well, that was cute and cozy." Bode frowned with his arms folded over his chest as he leaned against the kitchen counter.

I jumped when he spoke; I hadn't realized he was around. "Yeah, not so much."

Bode's frown deepened. "What's wrong. He do something?" He pushed from the counter as if preparing to chase Bruce and beat his face.

"Nothing like you're thinking." I shook my head. "No, just another classmate who wants all my notes, all my knowledge, all my effort on the homework and projects. If he could have asked me to take the damn test for him, he likely would have." I grabbed a soda from the fridge and popped it open. "You'd think I'd learn, but I always fall for it as if the next one will be different."

"Screw 'em. They don't deserve your help. Just say no. Say you've got to work, use me as an excuse, whatever." Bode all but flexed his muscles and pounded his chest. "You don't need them. Besides, he looked like a complete douche. He wasn't good enough for you."

I chuckled. "He was pretty douche-y. He only wanted my notes and work and study help. Would be one thing if he wanted to hang later, but he made it clear once he was here that he wasn't interested in being friends." I took a long swallow from the can of soda. "Did you think he was attractive?"

Bode wrinkled his nose. "Nah, not really. Probably his actions made him uglier to me than if he'd been a nice guy."

"Yeah." I took a deep breath. "I'm starving. You want pizza?"

"No, let's go down to the bar and fix something. I've got some new appetizers I want to try."

Benji and Kyson joined us and we hung out until the bar opened later in the evening. I couldn't remember when I'd ever had as much fun doing basically nothing as when I was with the guys. My heart sadly recalled how lonely I'd been before moving in with them. Having friends and belonging was definitely new to me, but it was something special that I never wanted to lose.

* * *

"Where are you going all spiffed up?" Bode asked when I stopped at the hall mirror to check my hair.

I ran my fingers through the blondish brown strands and tried to make them do what I wanted them to do. "Oh, um, I have a coffee date."

Benji and Kyson stuck their heads around the corner from the kitchen.

"Ohhh, that one guy on the app?" Benji pressed. "Tall, dark, handsome? What was his name?"

"You don't even know his name?" Bode demanded with a frown.

"His name is Casey. We've talked on the app a few times. He's coming here to pick me up and we're walking to Starbucks." I smiled despite feeling nervous. I wasn't completely sold on Casey, but he wasn't ugly and I figured it was worth at least giving him a chance.

"Whoa, whoa, whoa." Bode held his hands up in a protest gesture. "First off, the best place he can figure to take you is Starbucks? With all the great coffee on Mass. Ave., he chooses a lousy chain?" He shook his head.

I shrugged. "It's public and it's just coffee."

"And you're having this guy come *here* to pick you up? Letting him know where you live before you've even met him in person?" Bode scowled and threw a look toward Benji and Kyson. "Did you know about this?"

The guys shook their heads and grimaced.

I felt my stomach plummet. "Oh shit, that probably was a dumb idea, huh?" I bit my lip. "I'm sorry. He lives nearby and it made sense that he'd just swing by and pick me up on the way. I'll go downstairs and cut him off out front. That way he doesn't come up to the apartment."

Bode shook his head. "Negative. Let him come up.

We'll make sure he knows that you live with the three of us and he should promptly forget where you live if this date doesn't go well."

"Simple mistake, Sage." Benji smiled. "And, Bode," he gave his brother a pointed look, "there's nothing to say this date won't go wonderfully."

Bode grumbled.

I wondered briefly what it would be like if Bode was taking me on a coffee date. Would he be nervous? Would he hold doors for me? Would we have things to talk about? I knew he'd take me somewhere other than a chain store; Bode always wanted to support local small businesses. A flutter in my stomach responded as I once again thought of our kiss. I knew we'd agreed it was a mistake.

But it didn't *feel* like a mistake.

And was it a mistake if I wanted desperately for it to happen again?

A knock sounded at the door and Bode stalked toward it. He threw a glance over his shoulder toward Benji and Kyson as if to say *Get your asses over here*.

Benji rolled his eyes but put down the jewelry pieces he was working on. Kyson just smirked. They followed Bode to the door.

Bode yanked open the door. I assumed Casey was standing on the other side, but I couldn't see around my three roommates.

I watched in disbelief and amusement as Bode slowly wiped his hand on his pants before offering a hand shake. "I'm Bode. *One* of Sage's roommates and best friends." My heart soared as I heard him introduce himself and the guys as my best friends. I peeked around Kyson's shoulder and briefly saw Casey wince as he shook Bode's hand.

Benji and Kyson were introduced and I finally was allowed to step to the door to greet Casey.

"Hi." My face was hot. "So, you've met the roomies. You want to go?" I kinda just wanted to give him the boot and stay to hang with the guys. But I didn't want to be rude.

Casey eyed the guys suspiciously and nodded. "Yeah, let's get out of here."

"What time you think you'll be back?" Bode demanded from behind me.

When I turned to look at him he looked ferocious and my eyes grew wide. Heat flickered in my belly even as I tried to glare at him.

"What Bode means is have fun." Benji patted me on the shoulder.

Casey pulled me from the apartment and I heard arguing whispers as the door closed behind me.

"Sorry about that, my friends are just super protective." I followed Casey down the steps.

"Yeah, that was a bit much." Casey huffed but could barely pull his gaze from the shop windows. Was he checking himself out?

We made awkward small talk as we walked a couple blocks. If Casey's constant watching himself in windows like a damn bird wasn't bad enough, I definitely began to think the date was a possible dud within two minutes of arriving at the coffee shop. Casey stepped into line and bought himself a coffee without a word to me. I didn't expect him to treat, but we could have at least stood in line together. And *I* had been worried about being rude just moments before.

By the time I ordered and picked up my drink, Casey had found a table. He'd grabbed a napkin for himself and made himself comfortable in the cushy seat. Which left me to get my own napkin, move my hard wooden seat so it wasn't in the aisle and being blasted with direct sunlight, and toss the random magazine to the side.

Within a few minutes, I knew that not only was I right about the date being a dud, it was pretty much a disaster. I mean, nothing was spilled, I wasn't humiliated, and Casey wasn't a racist or bigot. But he was rude to me and others, slurped his coffee and made obnoxious humming noises the whole time he was enjoying his drink, and talked about himself non-stop. Like seriously, never stopped. I wasn't even sure he took a breath.

Once I'd finished my drink about an hour later, I'd done nothing but nod and add in the occasional *Mhm* to whatever Casey was babbling about. I surreptitiously glanced at my phone. I was ready to go. I couldn't take much more. I'd heard all about the random guys Casey had taken into empty rooms at the hotel where he worked as a night manager and how many girls he'd hooked up with before coming out as bi. He spoke incessantly about his cat and his bobblehead collection. Never once did he ask about me. Nothing about my schooling, my job, my hobbies, my friends. No, he prattled on about himself ad nauseam while continually glancing at his reflection in the window. I half expected him to make out with his shadow.

When Casey got up to go to the bathroom—well, that's where I assumed he went, he didn't actually excuse himself, just got up and walked away—I quickly shot a text to the guys.

In about five minutes, one of you needs to text me with a bar or apartment emergency so I can bow out of this nightmare coffee date. I'm not in trouble, just bored out of my mind because Casey is a self-centered, rude, egotistical asshole.

Before Casey returned, I'd gotten thumbs-up and *Gotcha* from my friends.

When he sauntered back from the bathroom and plopped down, I forced a smile and raised my brow. "I probably should be leaving soon. Bode or the guys will probably need my help."

"With what?" He threw out the question, but seemed to lose interest in my answer as soon as he caught his reflection in the window again.

My phone buzzed on the table and I picked it up in a rush, trying to appear nonchalant.

Get your ass back here and help in the bar. The mayo tubs exploded all over the back room and we need a major clean-up.

I nearly laughed out loud at the text, but I kept myself in check. "Oh, speak of the devil. It's Bode. He needs me at the bar. Mayo emergency. Duty calls."

"Mayo emergency? What the hell even is that?" Casey wrinkled his nose.

"A mess. Definitely a mess." I kept my face completely straight. "Bode's pissed and likely in mayonnaise up to his elbows." I stood.

Casey frowned. "So, what is that guy to you? Like are you into Daddy kink and shit?"

I snorted. "Bode is my landlord, boss, roommate, and friend. Anything beyond that is more complicated than either of us need it to be." *But you'd be oh so happy to take on the challenge of those complications, wouldn't you?* I cleared my throat. "I better head back." What else could I say? I enjoyed myself? Nice to meet you? Let's talk soon? None of those were honest words, so I gave him a weak smile, gathered my trash, and mumbled, "Take care," before rushing from the shop.

I all but ran home and up the stairs.

When I burst through the door, I expected to find the guys, but I only saw Bode.

A stressed and grumpy Bode who was deep in thought with papers strewn around him at the table.

"Mayo explosion, huh?" I kicked my shoes off.

We both chuckled.

"God, can you imagine what a mess that would be in reality?" Bode snorted.

"Where is everyone?"

"Kyson is hanging with Bay and Arlo. Benji went to that studio where he works on his artwork sometimes." Bode straightened from his slumped position and ran a hand over his face. "I know he'll be so glad to open his place and have his own studio to work on his pieces."

I walked over to where Bode was working. "What's wrong? You look stressed."

Bode laughed with no humor. "Am I ever *not* stressed lately?" He let his head fall into his hands and leaned his elbows on the table.

"What's up?" I sat next to him.

Bode gestured toward the papers. "Just numbers for the bar."

I picked up the paperwork and read through the figures. I frowned. "Bode, these reports show the Lizard made money, you're in the black. That's amazing after such a short time. Even looking at the projected numbers, they show a continued trend of profit and even an increased profit. Why are you stressed?"

Bode linked his hands at the crown of his head and sighed. "I'm cautiously optimistic and I feel really proud of the numbers." He paused and closed his eyes.

"But?"

"But I know it won't be good enough for my dad. He's already giving me shit, wanting to know numbers, asking for reports. I've been putting him off, but he'll visit soon I have no doubt. And he'll demand the reports. Put his nose where it doesn't belong." Bode huffed. "I appreciate the money he invested, but I hate that he acts as if it allows him to question everything and make demands. He's even hinting at things he wants to take a look at and changes he's assuming will need to be made."

"God, he's such an ass." I winced. "Sorry."

Bode chuckled. "No worries. It's the truth."

"Seriously, I can see where your stress is coming from, but he's not here right now. Take comfort in those numbers and let yourself breathe easy for a bit. You should be really proud." I put a hand on his arm.

Immediately a warmth traveled from my palm to my chest. When had this happened? When had I decided I was interested in Bode as more than just a hot ass to check out, fantasy fodder, or a good friend to spend time with? I couldn't recall an exact moment. But somewhere between Bode's hot and cold behavior and all of his protests regarding a relationship between us, my heart and body had made an executive decision and opted to desire something *more* with Bode.

I drew in a deep breath and let it out slowly. I should

have removed my hand from his arm, but Bode's breath caught and he stared at where our bodies connected before clenching his jaw and moving his gaze to my eyes.

"How was the coffee date? Was the douche bag as douche-y as I predicted?" Bode winked.

My cheeks grew hot and I wanted to protest, wanted to defend my choice, wanted Bode to be wrong. But he was so very right, I could only flop forward onto the table. "Thanks for the save. It was bad."

"Did he do something?" Bode immediately clicked into protective mode.

"Nothing *bad* bad. He just talked about himself incessantly, checked himself out in every shiny surface he could find, was rude to the wait staff, and pretty much treated me as an afterthought." I pushed myself up from the table and propped my head in my hand. "Honestly, I'm thinking *good, special, wonderful,* and *romantic* are words that I'll *never* get to use in regards to guys I go on dates with. I suck with making and keeping friends. I guess it's the same with guys." I pursed my lips and shrugged. "Lost cause."

Bode scowled. "No way." He shook his head. His eyes never left my face, traveling from my eyes to my lips and back to my eyes. Nostrils flaring, he gritted his teeth, closed his eyes, and let out a slow breath. "You *will* find something good, something special. You deserve romantic and wonderful, and one day you'll get it."

I smiled sadly. "I want to believe it, but I'm a twenty-four-year-old virgin with a number of dates I could count on fingers and one foot. The number of *good* dates fits only on fingers. And *any* sexual experiences with anyone other than myself add up to exactly two." I held up two fingers and stared at them. "It feels like I'm destined to study alone, sleep alone, and jack off alone." Before the words had barely left my lips, I blushed and groaned. "And embarrass myself with comments about jacking off alone." I let my head fall to the table again.

Bode laughed, but he seemed tense. "You'll get there. Any guy who can't see you for the amazing person you are is a total loser. And if they don't recognize how damn adorably cute and hot as fuck you are, they don't deserve a second glance."

My stomach fluttered and I swallowed thickly as I sat up and stared at Bode. We were so very close. The heat of his body blanketed mine and I could smell the faint hint of his soap and shampoo. Last time we were this close, Bode kissed me.

A mistake.

Just the stress.

Right.

I had to remember that Bode didn't feel the same about me as I realized I felt about him.

But that kiss had begged to differ.

Bode's lips and tongue had caressed, dipped, tasted, and teased as if he wanted to devour me. Did he kiss others like that if he didn't want anything more with them? If that was a *not interested* kiss, what would his *interested* kiss feel like? I wasn't sure I'd survive it.

Not that I'd ever get the chance to.

Bode wasn't interested.

He'd told that to me and anyone who would listen multiple times.

Then why was he still staring at my mouth? Why was

there a fire in his eyes? Why did his tongue wet his bottom lip as if remembering the taste of that kiss?

I stood abruptly from the table. "I need to go study." Rushing to my room, I pretended that I didn't hear Bode's request to come back. I needed to be away from him. Needed to calm my heart, my mind, and my body. Needed to be reminded that Bode was adamant we weren't a good fit.

I threw myself onto my bed, held my hands over my face and groaned.

* * *

About an hour later, I heard a knock on my door. I knew it was Bode. Neither Benji nor Kyson had come home from what I had heard from my hideout.

I swallowed my anxiety and anticipation and walked to the door.

Cracking the door, I peeped through the slight opening. "Uh, yeah?"

Bode offered a tentative smile. "Can I come in?"

"Oh, um," I stuttered. "I'm pretty tired, should probably study and get some rest." Why was I suddenly nervous about Bode? *Because he's probably going to tell you again how he's not interested and ask you to back off.*

"Please?" Bode's words were barely above a whisper. I'd never heard him so quiet. Never seen him appear so earnest.

Without a second thought, I stepped back and let the door swing open.

Bode took a step into my room and stopped right in front of me.

We stood there, facing each other, my cheeks warm and my heart pounding.

"I have something I need to say and I need you to just listen and not interrupt. Okay?" Bode's words poured from him in a rush.

I nodded.

Bode pushed the door closed behind him. "What I'm going to say is crazy and I don't know when it happened, but it's real and it's true and it's eating me alive."

I bit my lip and attempted to breathe normally.

"I still think you're too young for me. I'm scared shitless I'll mess something up. I'm terrified of not being enough for you, not being the right man to introduce you to sex. I'm not super patient, I'm hardheaded, I'm grumpy as fuck most of the time." Bode took a step toward me and cupped my jaw in his hand.

My heart nearly pounded out of my chest and I wasn't sure I was even breathing.

"But somewhere along the line I've had to admit, from the moment you knocked on our door all sweet and sexy, I've been fighting a losing battle." He caressed my cheek with his thumb. "That kiss in the bar wasn't a mistake. This isn't the stress talking. I want to kiss you again." He trailed his thumb across my bottom lip. "I want to kiss you every damn day and no matter how many times I tell myself it's not a smart move, I can't stop wanting to kiss you."

My breath audibly caught in my throat. I was frozen in place, my face and body on fire, my heart threatening to burst from my body, and my eyes glued to Bode's.

"Can I kiss you?" Bode's gaze moved to my lips. "Tell me no if you don't feel the same. It's probably for the best. I'll walk away and we can pretend this never happened."

"Do you want to pretend like it never happened?" My words were soft and raspy.

Bode shook his head. "No. My stubborn brain still thinks it's a bad idea, but I can't ignore this attraction any longer." He winced. "I know this is maybe coming out of left field, but I promise it's something I've been thinking about for a long time. I kept trying to push it away, but I can't." He moved closer, our bodies nearly touching from chest to knee. "When I heard you say you thought you'd never find something good in a guy, my gut and heart couldn't take it anymore. I'm scared I'm not *good* enough for you, but I'm tired of fighting it and I want to give it a chance." His eyes grew wide. "Unless you aren't feeling the same."

I smiled. "We're on the same page. I don't understand your attraction to me, but I definitely can't deny the fact that I find you hot as fuck. And despite your grumpiness, I'm drawn to you and find myself trying to spend time with you even if it doesn't make sense. I don't want to get ahead of myself, but there's *no* one I'd rather have introduce me to sex than you." I licked my lips and my dick twitched at the way Bode's eyes glowed when I mentioned sex. "So, I'm thinking you should kiss me. For real this time."

Bode shifted so that both hands could cup my face, tilted my head, tipped my chin up, and brushed his lips over mine so softly I almost thought I'd imagined the touch. Then he growled and captured my mouth with firm, silky lips, a warm tongue, and the rough scratch of stubble against my chin.

The taste of him on my tongue was like a hit for a drug addict. Just one taste would never be enough. I whimpered and opened my mouth wider in unmistakable invitation and wrapped my arms around him.

Bode kept his mouth on mine and lifted me from the floor in one swift motion. My legs went around his waist without hesitation. He turned and pressed my back against the door.

I broke from the kiss to suck in a ragged breath. "Oh God, Bode." My head fell against the door and my cock throbbed as Bode's mouth found my neck.

Bode's arms shook and his body shuddered under mine.

"Go to the bed," I demanded.

"Not sure that's smart." Bode panted and nuzzled his nose against my neck.

"I trust you. You'd never do anything I didn't want to do, right?"

He tensed. "Of course not. Never."

"Then take me to the bed."

Bode spun around and took three steps toward my bed. He placed me gently on the mattress and groaned as my thighs spread to take his hips between my legs. He captured my mouth again and we kissed for several blissful moments while rocking our hips together.

Finally, I pulled back and took a deep breath. "Okay, we should probably stop before our first real kiss ends up leading to our first sexual encounter."

"Oh God." Bode groaned and maneuvered our bodies to lay long-ways on the bed before rolling off me. "I'm sorry, was that too much?"

I smiled and cuddled into him. "Not at all."

We laid together in a comfortable silence for a moment before I propped up on my elbow.

"Are we really doing this?"

Bode snorted. "Well, we *really did* that kiss." But his eyes were serious. "I want to. It's crazy and maybe it's a bad move, but I'm so tired of pushing the feelings away and trying to convince myself I don't find myself attracted to you. If you didn't feel the same, I'd ignore it and move on. But, if you're feeling the same, I feel like we owe it to ourselves to at least give it a try." He smirked and cupped my cheek.

"I feel the same." I leaned into his touch. "So, what do we do now?"

"You okay with just laying here while I hold you and we kinda gather our thoughts?"

I nodded and cuddled into his chest. Was this really happening? Surely I was asleep and dreaming; I'd wake up soon.

About thirty minutes later, we had dozed a bit and just enjoyed being close.

Bode shifted so we were better positioned to talk. "You want to discuss anything?"

So, not a dream. This was real.

"Want to start with concerns?" I ran my hand down Bode's arm and took his hand.

He took a deep breath and nodded. "I think the age thing is one of my biggest concerns."

I smiled softly. "It's ten years. That's not really *that* much." I squeezed his hand. "I'm not sure if anything will grow from the attraction between Kyson and Bay, but are you concerned about that fourteen-year gap?"

Bode seemed to mull that over before shaking his

head. "No. I guess it's because Ky's my age so he doesn't seem as young to me."

"Does Bay seem too old for him?"

"No. I don't see the age difference being that noticeable between them." He frowned. "I guess I really don't know why it feels like such a big deal between us."

"I don't know either. It's not like I'm *barely legal*. I've been living on my own for a while. I'm an intelligent person. I'm well-educated and resourceful. I'm not just a kid."

Bode nodded. "I'll try to work on the way I frame our age difference in my head." He leaned close and kissed me. "Your turn for a concern."

I pursed my lips. "Well, I have a couple. I'll start with the biggest one."

Bode raised a brow and waited.

"You run so hot and cold with me. You're always protective and a friend, but you've been on and off with the way you act toward me so much." I nibbled on my lip. "I guess I'm worried this is just one of those hot or on moments and soon you'll be back to denying there's anything between us."

Bode sighed. "I can understand that. I guess I was so convinced that we weren't good for each other and I wanted to be the good guy and do right by you."

A flicker of irritation flamed. "I've said this so many times. I'm a grown man. Maybe I haven't lived as many years as you, but *I* should get a say in what's *right* for me."

"I get that. I do." Bode nodded. "And I'm sorry."

"Your turn." I brought our clasped hands to my chest.

"I'm fucking scared to death of hurting you. I've never taught someone to have sex. What if I fuck it up? What if

I scar you for life?" Bode's gruff words were laced with real worry.

I couldn't help but smile. "My parents scarred me for life. My terrible dating history is fucked up. I can assure you that I don't need to be *taught* how to have sex. Just because I'm not experienced doesn't mean I don't know the ins and outs. Again, I'm a big boy. I'm well-versed in positions, preparations, precautions, and plenty of porn."

Bode laughed. "My little alliterator." He kissed me gently.

"Is alliterator even a word?" I narrowed my eyes.

He shrugged. "It is now. Tell me more about these positions, preparations, precautions, and porn."

My cheeks heated. "Well, I've watched plenty of porn. The good *and* the bad. I know positions I want to try. Preparations as far as cleaning and stretching; I think using a butt plug sounds sexy as hell."

Bode groaned and leaned in to kiss me.

I laughed. "Note to self: Bode likes the idea of me using a butt plug."

"Bode likes that idea very much. But go on."

"Precautions like condoms and testing. I've been tested. I'm negative for any type of STI. If my partner were to also be negative and we were monogamous, I'd be willing and interested in going bare."

Bode's eyes went wide.

"And I've had several years of touching myself to learn what I like. Just because I've had limited sexual experience with others doesn't mean I'm not familiar with sex. And I may have never had an actual dick in my ass, but toys are fun and do the job very well." I finished my little speech and thought my face would catch fire. I buried my head in Bode's chest. "And I can't believe I just said all of that."

He chuckled and lifted my face. "No, I'm glad you did. I had it in my mind that you were a sheltered, inexperienced, innocent virgin—and I'm not saying there's a single thing wrong with that—but knowing you're so in touch with your sexual desires makes me a little less anxious."

"Yeah, eight years ago, I was a whole different story. But I'm a learner, I thrive on preparing and researching. So, it makes sense that I'd delve into learning about my sexual likes and wishes with or without a partner."

"Eight years ago, you were sixteen so let's not ever refer to that and sex ever again." Bode chucked my chin. "What are your thoughts on a sexual relationship between us?"

"Yes, please." I teased. "No, seriously. If we're both comfortable with it, I'd like to move into a physical relationship fairly quickly. I'm old enough to know what I want. I'm not saying I want to jump you tonight, but I don't think we need to wait for a prolonged period; it's not like we don't know each other fairly well already."

Bode nodded. "Okay, I can see that. And you won't get any complaints from me." His lips twisted. "What was your other concern?"

I rolled on top of him and repositioned our bodies so we were laying on our opposite sides. Drawing in a deep breath, I let it out slowly and shook my head in disbelief. "Um, before I get to that, does this seem absolutely insane and surreal?"

"You mean the fact we've known each other for this long and we've danced around our feelings and attraction with protests and excuses and hiding? And now we're kissing, talking about sex, and cuddled in bed together?" Bode raised his brow.

I nodded and a kinda crazy laughter escaped. "Well, at least *one* of us has hidden his feelings with protests and excuses." I ran my hand up Bode's chest.

"You're right. That's mostly on me. But yes, it does seem a little insane and surreal." Bode wrapped an arm around me and pulled me close. "But it also seems like the best decision I've made in a long time and I feel so right and at peace with it. Like holding you and kissing you is the most natural thing in the world and it's what's been missing in my life. What about you?"

I bit my lip and blinked back the sting of tears. "Same. I'd convinced myself that I was blessed to just have the three of you as friends and I'd just have to ogle you from afar. But this is so much better. I know it's not guaranteed forever, but I'm excited to see where it goes."

"So, your other concern?"

I pursed my lips. "I guess there's a tiny part of myself that worries we'll crash and burn and I'll lose my three best friends, a home, and a job."

Bode rested his forehead against mine. "God, that's one of my biggest fears. I know how things can get fucked up in a messy break up. But let's promise right now that we'll do everything in our power to keep the friendships intact. We were friends before this, we can at least try to be friends if we decide it's not meant to be anything more."

I took a shuddery breath. "Agreed."

"Have we talked ourselves out or do you have other questions?"

I thought for a moment. "I guess I'm just wondering what triggered you to make this move."

Bode worried his bottom lip with gleaming white teeth and soothed the bite with his tongue before he spoke. "The main thing is that there's this crazy attraction between us—and I need you to know it's not just physical—and I was already failing trying to convince myself it was best to ignore the attraction. Then when you said you thought you'd never find a good guy, it broke me. I want to be that for you. I'm not sure I *can* be that for you, but I want to try."

"What else? That's the *main* reason, but was there something else?"

"This one is harder to explain. It has to do with my father."

I couldn't help my eyes going wide, but I kept my mouth shut.

"He's so negative, so against anything that may upset his perfect reputation and life. He's constantly running down my hopes and dreams." Bode frowned. "It hit me recently that *I* was turning into him. I was being so negative toward anything that may have been building between us. I was against the age difference, the difference in our personalities and education levels. In reality, I was beginning to run down my own hopes and dreams. That realization hit me like a bucket of ice water and I promised myself I'd turn it around and *not* be like him. The first thing that came to mind was being open and positive and hopeful about whatever may be growing between us." He pulled me close and held me. "If any of that makes sense."

I nodded. "It does. It makes a lot of sense actually." I kissed his cheek. "So where do we go from here?"

"I think we tell the guys we're giving this a shot. And we do the official dating thing."

"Can dating and sex coincide?" I lifted a brow.

"So eager," Bode teased. "I think since we live together and have had a lot of time to get to know each other, we can ease into dating *and* sex simultaneously."

"Sounds perfect." I kissed him. "You know Ky and Benji are going to give you so much shit."

Bode held a finger to my lips. "Shhhh, don't remind me."

We laid silent and comfortable for several moments.

"Oh, here's a question. If we're dating, I think I should know your full name." I cupped his jaw with my hand.

Bode snorted. "My full name is Boden Flynn Silver. Flynn is my mom's middle name. Benji and I couldn't say *Boden* very well when we were little, so it got shortened to *Bo-dee* and stuck. What about you?"

"Sage Maxwell Holder." I smiled. "Pleased to meet you. Now I think we should get naked."

Bode's eyes went wide. "Um, I think an official date is needed before sex."

I rolled my eyes. "I'm not talking full-on penetrative sex. But naked cuddling isn't asking too much is it?"

Bode sat up and pulled his shirt over his head. "Get naked."

When we were sans clothing, we fell back into bed and spent several moments kissing, tasting, and teasing. Soon though, Bode rolled on top of me and settled between my legs. Our throbbing cocks met and a jolt of heat traveled between our bodies.

"Oh God, Bode." I moaned and rocked my hips into his.

"Sage, you are so gorgeous and you feel so damn good. I could totally come this way." Bode kissed my neck and rolled his hips against mine.

"Do it. I want to come with you on top of me like this, our cocks pressed together." I ran my hands down his back and gripped his ass. "Thrust against me just like you'll do when you're fucking me."

Bode groaned and began thrusting his hips against mine in a slow, sensual rhythm. Hard, hot dicks rubbed together, heavy balls pressed close, and my body ached to open for him. All too soon my release erupted between us followed almost immediately by Bode's as he painted my belly in sticky spurts.

We lay together breathing heavily for a long moment before he kissed me.

"Was that okay?" he asked, uncertainty evident in his voice.

"That was so amazingly okay." I kissed him deeply. "Stay?"

Bode smiled and nodded with heavy eyes. He rolled from bed and grabbed a washcloth from the bathroom. After he wiped us both clean, he tossed the cloth to the floor and climbed back in bed with me. We quickly fell into an easy and comfortable sleep.

11

BODE

"WHATEVER IN THE world do you think may have happened?" A staged whisper mocked and intruded into my sleep.

"He said it wouldn't work. *We're too different, he's too young, he's our renter.*" Another whisper joined in the performance.

I buried my head into the pillow, my chin nuzzling the top of Sage's head. Cracking an eye, I confirmed that both my asshole brother and cousin were plopped on the end of Sage's bed grinning at me like damn loons.

I gently lifted my arm from around Sage's waist and flipped them the bird.

Sage shifted and chuckled. "I told you they were going to give you so much shit."

"Can you two stop being voyeuristic perverts and get out of here?" I wouldn't turn down another few minutes of sleep with Sage in my arms.

"No can do, brother." Benji grabbed my calf and squeezed.

"Ow! Why not?" I scowled as I rolled to my back and propped my head on my bent arm.

Sage did the same.

What a picture we must have been. Not only rumpled and shirtless, but completely naked under the sheets. Not that they needed to know that. But I'm sure they had an idea.

My cock stirred at the thought of naked Sage. No, no, no. I did *not* need to be tenting the sheet in front of Benji and Kyson.

"Well, you see, we're slightly concerned about this turn of events." Kyson grinned from his perch on the end of the bed.

I raised a brow.

Benji leaned closer and pretended to whisper. "Did Sage force himself on you? Did he take advantage of you? Make you go against all of your protests and excuses? Tell us, brother. We'll help you; we'll save you from his advances."

Sage snorted.

"Will you two knock it off?" I growled and ran a hand over my face.

"Wait, you don't mean…" Kyson let his words trail off and made a big deal of looking surprised. "Do you mean to tell me that you—big, bad, grumpy, gruff Bode who swore nothing could happen between him and sweet, sexy Sage—you're telling me that my dear cousin finally pulled his head from his ass and admitted that all of his protests and excuses were worthless?"

Benji slapped his hands against his cheeks and his mouth opened into an O. "What? No!" He glanced a Sage.

"Wait, should we be concerned about Sage? Did Bode take advantage of you?"

"Oh my God," I groaned.

Sage laughed. "No. I promise this is mutual."

"Well then, I think Benji and I have a job to do." Kyson nodded with a wicked grin.

I narrowed my eyes. "What?"

"First, is this just sex or is it more serious?" Benji held his hand up to pause the conversation before they explained further.

I glanced at Sage and we both smiled. "More serious is the plan."

"So, like officially dating?" Kyson clarified.

Sage and I both nodded.

"Okay, then we definitely have to follow through on a promise we made Sage." Benji leaned against the wall and put his legs over mine. "We told Sage we'd check out any guys he might date and offer him pointers." He grinned.

Kyson was still smiling from ear-to-ear. "Let's start with a physical once over."

I groaned.

Sage hooked an arm through mine and cuddled close. "Oh, yes. I definitely don't have the dating experience to know if I'm making a good choice. Please give me all your tips, insight, and advice." He ran a hand over my chest and smiled at me.

"What happened to you being a grown-up who can make your own damn choices?" I grumbled, but the whole situation had a good-natured vibe and I loved that the four of us were close enough that something like this could happen without any weirdness.

"Eh, I feel I should hear them out. Weigh my options."

"Well, you're in luck that both Benji and I have years of experience with this specific model of man and we can speak with much knowledge of all of his attributes." Kyson gestured toward me with a flourish. "We have a fairly fine specimen here if we're judging just based on physical attributes. If you like a beefcake, however, you're out of luck with this one." Kyson held his chin in his hand and pretended to critique me from head to toe. "If you prefer more of the twink look, this one doesn't fit the bill either. But if you're interested in the strong, lean muscular swimmer-type build, this model will fulfill your wishes."

"Although, the hair is often in an annoyingly perfect imperfection that may draw your jealousy if you struggle with your own coiffure. And the shit-eating grin can sometimes rub one the wrong way, especially if you're already irritated." Benji acted as if these were negatives. "But he has the standard, yet well-liked, brown hair and hazel eyes along with a 6'3" frame. However, there is the issue of a slight scar on his eyebrow from a fight with Kyson at age ten."

I laughed. Damn hair never did grow back in that one small area of my brow.

"Oh, in the interest of total transparency, we must disclose that this model has had several complaints about volume control. Seems to get stuck in *loud* and *too fucking loud* a lot of the time." Kyson frowned. "It's a factory flaw."

I rolled my eyes and snorted.

"As far as the non-physical attributes, this model you've opted for has a lot of positives." Benji rubbed his hands together.

"But we'd remiss not to also mention the negatives." Kyson nodded sagely.

"This design is extremely loyal, determined, a hard worker, and the life of any party. Overcame a lot in school and is conquering successes left and right." Benji placed a hand on my leg and my heart warmed at my brother's words. Benji and Kyson knew how much of a challenge school was for me.

"This particular prototype *does* have some functionality issues. First, he works too much and too late and ends up sleeping in way too long most days." Kyson started numbering my flaws on his hand. "He gets too down on himself a lot of the time. He's also grumpy and gruff and stubborn as hell, but I see you may have already realized and moved past this aspect of his personality." Ky winked.

"Overall, if you're looking for our recommendation," Benji started, but paused and looked at Sage who nodded in affirmative. "We'd say this specimen comes highly recommended and our prediction is that you'll be very happy with him."

Sage cuddled even closer. "Wow, that was a lot of insight. I'm going to guess you wouldn't have been so thorough with anyone else. Guess it's a good thing you're well-acquainted with my current crush."

I jostled Sage. "Current, huh? So, I'll just be one of many in a long string of guys you love and leave?" I teased.

Sage blushed. "Not like that." He buried his head in my chest.

"You guys have any insights for me on Sage? Maybe I should reconsider." I winked at Sage.

"Oh, this model is sublime." Kyson shook his head as

if in awe. "A true one of a kind. Intelligent, gorgeous green eyes and light brown hair, measuring in at a respectable 5'9". This model is top level in the twinkish build category. Long, lean, slim frame. Overcame a lot of bullshit from his parents; you two make a great match in that aspect."

"Not without his own flaws, this prototype *does* bite his nails and doesn't realize how great he is. You'll need to be patient with him due to some social awkwardness." Benji gave Sage a soft smile and a wink.

"Well, this has been extremely enlightening and all, but could you two scram now?" I needed to piss and I wanted some time with Sage before we had to start our day.

Benji and Kyson stood from the bed.

"Seriously, we're happy for you both. Neither of us see this as a mistake." Benji gestured toward where Sage and I laid in the bed.

"Very happy for you. This is going to be a good thing." Kyson smiled.

My brother and cousin left the room.

I rolled to Sage. "Well, that was fun."

Sage chuckled. "Mmhm." He ran his hand over my chest. "You wanna shower before we have to return to reality?"

I pulled him close and nuzzled his neck. "Naked with you in the shower to start my day? Yes, please."

We rolled from bed and my dick sprang to life as I watched Sage's sweet ass saunter to the bathroom with a *come-hither* look thrown over his shoulder. Had I missed his flirty side or was I so busy denying there was anything between us that I refused to see it? Or maybe Sage had been holding back too?

Taking this step and admitting my attraction and feelings toward him was somewhat sudden and scary as fuck even though it wasn't like I just woke up and acted on the feelings; I'd been at war with my head and heart for several weeks. But everything about it—whatever was possibly growing between us—once I'd allowed myself to concede defeat and acknowledge the attraction and feelings weren't going away and weren't *wrong*, seemed so very right and natural. It was as if we'd been destined to eventually get to this point, I was just too stubborn to see it for a while. Now I was privileged to get to know Sage as more than a friend. And my heart was so on-board with the turn of events.

I closed both bathroom doors and switched on the vent fan before turning on the water.

Sage put toothpaste on both of our toothbrushes and handed mine to me. "I plan on being very up close and personal, banish the morning breath."

We both made a quick job of brushing our teeth.

I took a piss and kissed Sage soundly before climbing in the shower. "Take a leak if you need to, I'm not into water sports so no pissing on my feet in there."

He laughed.

While Sage used the bathroom, I soaped my dick and ass in hopes at least one would be getting action. When Sage pulled back the curtain and stepped in, I was soaping my armpits and chest. We each washed our hair and bodies quickly before abandoning the soap and taking each other in our arms.

"Good morning," I murmured against Sage's minty-fresh lips.

"Good morning." Sage licked at my lips and rolled his hips against mine as if I needed a reminder that our rock hard cocks were pressed together and begging for attention.

"What do you want to do?" I trailed my hands down his back and gripped his perfect ass cheeks.

When Sage dropped his head back and exposed his neck, I couldn't help but devour the sensitive skin and take extreme pleasure in the whimpers and moans escaping him as I kissed, nipped, and licked.

"I want to suck you." He panted and rocked his hips again. "But this is where I'm seriously inexperienced. I've had things in my ass, but I don't have a lot of blow job experience."

I brought my hands up to cup his face. "Your mouth on my cock, even just the *thought* of you sucking me, is enough to have me busting a nut. I can promise you that any sucking you choose to do will be much appreciated."

Sage blushed. "I guess I'm just worried that you've been with so many guys and I'll pale in comparison."

"Hey," I whispered. "I've not been with *that* many guys, but I guarantee that every single one of them pales in comparison to you. You're gorgeous, you're so damn smart and good, and you're one of my closest friends. I don't know how our relationship grew so fast and easy, but nothing I ever had with any of them can compare to what we have together." I kissed him then and hoped the sincerity of my words was evident in the way my tongue mated with his. It was odd to see Sage so unsure of himself when he was usually the one in the know about everything. My heart simultaneously warmed and clenched at the thought that *I* would be the one at the head of the class in this situation. "And once you blow me, I'm taking my turn because I can't wait to take this beautiful cock deep in my throat and swallow everything you can give me." I stroked him in my wet fist.

Sage sagged against me with a moan before dropping to his knees. He took my cock in his hand and those big, green eyes trailed up my body before meeting mine. He licked his lips and smiled shyly.

"Do whatever you want. Anything you do will be perfect." I meant every word I said. But I was going to die from the anticipation if he didn't do something soon.

But Sage saved me. And, oh God, he did something. Something so good. His pretty pink tongue flicked out from between plump lips and teased at my slit before circling the head. When he stopped teasing and opened wide to take me in, I slapped my hands against the tiles before gripping my hair and groaning. I wanted to grab Sage's head and fuck his face, but I fought to control the urge.

Sage sucked me deep, pressing his tongue flat and then stroking my length with his lips and fist. "Pull my hair." His demand was muffled as he spoke around my cock stuffed in his mouth, but I heard him loud and clear.

Without argument, I ran my hands through his hair. Gently at first and then a bit rougher.

"*Pull* it."

My man knew what he wanted. I took a fistful of his pretty hair and yanked it. Not enough to truly hurt, but enough that I knew it likely stung.

Sage groaned around my dick and gripped my ass as he

thrust my cock in and out of his mouth in a hard and fast rhythm. When his fingers found my hole and teased, I knew I wouldn't last much longer. My balls drew up tight with even that slight ass play and I pulled Sage's hair tighter. When he pushed a warm, wet finger against my hole, I lost any semblance of control and shot hot spurts deep in his waiting mouth.

I opened my eyes to watch as his greedy throat convulsed around my load while his gaze never left mine. So fucking hot.

I let go of his hair and pulled him up. My mouth captured his and devoured him with long, strong thrusts of my tongue. The taste of me on his tongue was a heady treat. "That was amazing. You are a gorgeous and superbly talented little cocksucker." I kissed him again as he blushed and laughed. "My turn. Let's see if I can follow that performance."

I dropped to my knees and nuzzled my nose against the light brown pubic hair.

Sage gripped his cock and pressed it against my cheek. "As close as I came to blowing my load along with you, I don't think you're going to have much trouble getting me off whether you match my skills or not."

I swallowed him whole and teased one finger against his hole and cupped his balls with my other hand. I let him fuck my face, his long dick hitting the back of my throat as his balls bumped my chin. When he put his hands on the tile above my head, I pulled off momentarily. "Fuck my mouth. Fuck me until you come."

Sage groaned and did exactly that.

When his cock erupted in my mouth, I swallowed every drop until he slowed and pulled his softening length from between my lips. I stood quickly and pressed him against the wall before kissing him, thrusting my tongue deep in his mouth, making sure he could taste himself on my lips.

"That was so damn hot," Sage murmured against my mouth. "Can we shower like this every morning?"

I laughed. "Well, I'll have to up your rent to cover our water bill, but I think it would be worth it."

"Totally worth it." Sage kissed me. "Thank you for that. It was so good. Did I do okay?"

My eyes widened. "Are you serious? That was quite possibly one of the best blow jobs I've ever gotten." What he lacked in experience and skill he totally made up for in enthusiasm and effort.

He blushed and kissed me as the water began to run cold.

"You want to have our first official date tomorrow? Maybe brunch and a day out before I need to be back here to open the bar at six?"

"Sounds good. I'm going to study and head to the library for a while today. I'll be down later tonight to help at the bar." Sage kissed me before reaching behind me to turn off the water.

"Okay." I climbed from the shower. "Oh, before I forget. If we're sleeping together tonight, I vote for my bed. It's bigger." I didn't plan on anything more than blowjobs and maybe some ass play for a while, but I definitely wanted a bigger bed no matter what. And a small caveman-ish part of me beat on his chest thinking about bringing Sage into *my* bed and making him mine.

An hour later, I was busy finalizing some paperwork in

my office downstairs when Benji popped his head around the corner.

"Hey man, you got a minute?" Leave it to my brother to ask that question as he barged right on in and took a seat.

"Sure, come in. Make yourself at home." I smirked. "What's up?"

"Everything is cleaned and stocked up front. Ky's finishing up in the kitchen."

"Okay, thanks." I put my pen down. "But what are you really here to talk about?"

Benji grinned. "Don't go acting like you can read my mind with some twin-voodoo-shit."

I laughed. "Nothing like that, but I've known you for thirty-four years. I know when you've got something on your mind. Have you met someone? I noticed you've been out late a couple nights lately." I knew Benji wanted something serious, but had a history of casual sex and fun dates that never really led anywhere. He always said that he was enjoying the fun, but every so often he'd admit that he was feeling ready for something more.

"Nah, just a few dates and sex here and there." He shrugged.

"Good on both accounts?" I raised a brow.

Benji nodded. "Definitely."

"So, what's up?"

"Sage."

My chest tightened. "What's wrong with Sage?"

Benji smiled. "Nothing. He's great. And you seem to finally be admitting that as well."

I sighed. Dating or not, I'd felt protective of Sage since

day one. "Yeah, guess I finally pulled my head from my ass."

"Why the change of heart?"

I leaned back in my chair. "Honestly, I don't think my heart changed. If I'm being one hundred percent truthful, I've felt something for him since that first day we interviewed him. I just wouldn't admit or accept it, so I pushed and protested. But yeah, there's definitely something there." I smiled at the thought of Sage.

"I'm surprised you didn't talk to me or Ky." Benji cocked his head.

I mulled that over for a while. "Yeah, I guess I was being my usual stubborn self and didn't want to admit it to you guys since you'd been seeing something between us from the beginning."

"Don't get me wrong. I'm thrilled you guys are going to give it a shot, but you're not usually one to admit when you're wrong so easily. What pushed you to the decision?" Benji crossed an ankle over his knee. He was dusty so I knew he'd been working with clay in the studio. Probably earrings or figurines or vases.

I shared the story of Sage being bummed about his date and then saying that he didn't think he'd ever find a good guy, the right guy, and how I couldn't help but want to be that for him. And then I brought up the part our dad played in my decision.

"I just don't ever want to be like him. The best way to be exactly the opposite of him was to open myself up, admit my feelings, and let something good happen. Something good that I'm not doing for professional gain or financial reasons, just letting something good take root because it feels natural and right." I smiled softly and ran a hand over my face. "Sage is so sweet and sexy, so smart and good. I know I've said *good* like a million times, but that's what he is, how he makes me feel."

"I'm so happy for you, Bo." Benji stood up and walked around my desk to pull me into a hug. "He's an amazing guy. Glad we vetoed your vote way back when we were looking for a renter."

"Me too." I hugged him back. "But this doesn't mean you guys get to veto all of my votes."

Benji slapped me on the back. "Mhmm, we'll see." He laughed and gave me a wave as he left my office.

The morning of our date, at a few minutes before eleven o'clock, Sage and I headed down the stairs and walked to Rooster's Kitchen for lunch. Sage chose a pork sandwich with a smoky cheese, mustard, and pickles. He shared it with me so he could have some of my *build your own* macaroni and cheese with pulled pork, broccoli, and a crusty coating of potato chips. We shared a delicious portion of bread pudding for dessert.

As we walked and enjoyed the sunshine, Sage took my hand. "Is this okay?"

"Absolutely. So, let's do questions. What's one thing about growing up that sucked for you? Aside from your parents?" I didn't like bringing up bad shit, but I wanted to know everything about him.

"Ugh, homophobic assholes for sure. I was bullied in school for being a scrawny, gay nerd. And hell, that was before they even knew I was gay." Sage wrinkled his nose. "But I've always loved learning, so I used my knowledge as a shield and a way to beat them. My intelligence was another isolating factor when it came to having friends, but at least it allowed me to grow and succeed. I soared past them and never looked back. What about you?"

"Yeah, homophobic assholes for me too. But having Benji and Kyson on my side helped ease that issue a little. Honestly, even more so than that, was reading. Reading was so hard for me in school that I sometimes wondered if I'd actually graduate. My dad would never allow me to get special tutoring because he thought it made me look stupid. Luckily, a teacher in middle school recognized my struggles came from a form of dyslexia. She asked my parents if she could help me at school. My dad refused, but my mom contacted the teacher later and gave permission. I used my study hall to get extra help. I don't turn letters around, I have surface dyslexia so words that aren't pronounced the way they look are difficult for me. But I made huge strides in middle school and continued getting help in high school and reading got a little easier each year. I also researched and worked on my reading at home. I have a lot of bad feelings toward reading still, but I'm a pretty decent reader these days compared to how much I used to struggle. It's taken me a long time to come to grips with my struggles not meaning I'm dumb or can't learn. When I started making progress in school, it was like I finally started to believe that maybe I wasn't stupid." I clenched my jaw after that sordid story poured from me. I shook my head. "I think my struggles in school and your extreme intelligence were kinda one of the reasons I fought *us* so much. I hate feeling dumb in comparison to other people."

Sage squeezed my hand. "Never. You're one of the

smartest people I've ever known. You've got a gift when it comes to people and business. If I've ever made you feel less than me, please forgive me."

"Not a single time. The fear was just in my head." I shook my head. "What's a fear you have?"

Sage thought for a moment. "The fear of not knowing something or not being able to learn. I also fear, maybe loathe is a better word, deception. Being kept out of the loop or lied to is one of the worst things a person can do to me. My parents never shared anything with me and they lied to me a lot. I hate being deceived. What about you?"

I frowned. "I mean, I hate worms thanks to Kyson putting a handful of them down my shirt." I pointed to the scar on my eyebrow. "That's where this came from. But in terms of big fear? I think being knocked down, overthrown. Like my dad coming in and taking away everything I've worked for."

Sage sighed as we entered Global Gifts. "We should both maybe think about seeing a mental health professional." He chuckled.

I joined in. But he wasn't wrong.

We browsed the store and enjoyed their unique items. I saw a couple things I'd maybe come back and buy for Sage one day. We said goodbye to the friendly employee and continued our wandering. Leaving the more serious chatter behind, we spoke of the great bars and restaurants on Mass. Ave. and decided the four of us needed to head over a few blocks to 16-Bit Arcade one day soon.

"Oh my gosh, I'd never even thought of it, but this is totally your store." Sage came to a dead stop and pointed at a storefront. "It's exactly what you guys are."

I laughed as I read the store's name. Silver in the City. "Yeah, I guess you're right. I mean, they sell fun, unconventional gifts and great Indiana and Indianapolis items while the three of us are just here to build and conquer our dreams. But the name does fit."

We spent the next thirty minutes roaming the store and laughing about some of the amazing gift options. Sage bought a couple pairs of funny socks and I got a t-shirt with Indiana as a frothy beer mug. The store was always a great place for fun purchases.

By the time we reached Pumkinfish, we decided we were about done shopping. So, we browsed the eclectic collection the store had to offer and headed back the way we'd come.

A few blocks later, we popped into Mass. Ave. Wine and enjoyed a wine tasting along with warm bread and dipping oil before heading back home.

After a nap, we went downstairs to open the bar and had one of the busiest Sunday nights at the bar we'd ever had.

When Sage and I climbed into my bed after a quick shared shower later that night, I sighed contentedly. "This has been one of the best days I've had in a very long time." I kissed the top of his head.

"Same." Sage cuddled against my side.

The fact that we were nearly naked in bed and cuddling felt just as natural and right as if we'd been doing anything of a sexual nature screamed at me how different things between Sage and I were in comparison to other men I'd had in my bed. They had been quick and easy and casual. Sage was so much more.

* * *

"I kinda like waking up with you in my bed." I nuzzled against Sage's neck and pulled his back tight against my chest the next morning.

"And I kinda like waking up in your bed." Sage stretched and arched his back so his ass pressed against my morning erection. "You were right, the bigger bed is a lot more comfortable for two people."

"Mmhm," I growled against his ear. "And you're a bed hog."

Sage gasped. "How dare you!" He laughed and wrestled with me until I pinned him down.

With one hand, I held his wrists above his head and trailed my other hand softly down his bare chest. "I seem to remember a certain tick check moment and it reminds me of the fact that you're ticklish."

Sage wiggled under me. "No, please." He squealed as my fingers tickled along his armpit and down his side.

"But I've got you trapped in my bed, what else could we possibly do other than tickle fights?" I teased and slowed my tickling fingers to rub gently over Sage's pebbled nipples.

His breath caught and he bit his lip. "I think I have an idea."

When I released his wrists, his hands immediately trailed down my chest to the sheet wrapped around my waist. I watched and barely breathed as his fingers teased at the sheet.

"What's your idea?" My words were gravely and my heartbeat had increased tenfold.

"You'll need to roll to your back." The heat in Sage's eyes spurred me on.

I moved from straddling him to my back and put my hands behind my head. "As long as this isn't just a ruse to escape."

Sage smirked and moved atop me, straddling me. "I'd be crazy to leave this." He shifted and pulled the sheets from under and around us. His bare skin was now warm against mine and all teasing thoughts were gone. Sage glanced toward the table next to my bed. "You have lube in there?"

I nodded. Surely he wasn't…

He leaned over, nearly toppling from the bed, and I gripped his hips to steady him. Sage returned with the lube and a triumphant smile.

"What are you—" I started, but Sage put a finger to my lips.

"Just enjoy. I'm not doing anything I don't want to do. If you don't like it, you can tell me to stop." He moved so he was on my thighs and dribbled lube on my hard and heavy cock.

"It involves you, naked, and lube. I think I'll love it." I bucked my hips a bit in a silent request for Sage to touch me.

He poured a small amount of the liquid on his finger and, never taking his eyes from mine, reached behind to slick his ass. "I ordered a butt plug. I think I'll start teasing you by wearing it to random outings just so you know I'm getting my ass ready for you."

My hips jerked and he slid forward. "Dear God, Sage, you're gonna kill me talking like that. Would you really do that? Slide a thick plug in your ass and tease me with it?"

The knowledge would have me on edge all day, but the pleasure we'd find later would be oh so worth it.

"Not only would I totally prep my body with a butt plug and tease you with the information, I'd be thinking about it being your big, fat cock all day long." He maneuvered himself on my body, legs spread around my waist, and settled his ass over my cock, wiggling until his cheeks were spread and engulfing my slick dick.

I groaned at both the promise in his words and the heat of his ass hugging my cock.

"Soon, you'll be stretching me wide and filling my hole with that gorgeous cock of yours." Sage rocked his hips and allowed my length to slide slowly through his slick crack. "Until then, I'm going to ride you just like this until we both come. You okay with that?"

I nodded and gripped his hips. "I want you to jerk yourself off and come all over me."

Sage groaned and continued rocking his hips and sliding his ass over my slick cock while he took himself in his fist and stroked. His hot ass gripped my dick and I gasped when he moved a hand behind him and between my legs to fondle my balls. "Slide your cock against my hole while I jack myself."

His demand went straight to my nuts and I thrust hard through his warm, slick ass cheeks until my shaft hit his balls.

"Oh fuck, yeah. Just like that. Do it again." He kept playing with my balls as he stroked his cock.

With my hands on his hips, I continued to slide my dick against his hole. I lost all semblance of control when Sage brought a finger to his mouth, slicked it with spit, and trailed the wetness along my taint until he pressed against my hole. My balls tightened and I shot my hot load into his crack and onto his balls.

Sage moaned and dropped to his elbows so our chests were flush together. He kissed me deeply, his tongue rutting against mine just as his cock rubbed against mine.

I took advantage of the new position to trail my fingers against his wet, sticky hole. I pressed gently until my gorgeous boy opened for my slick finger. "Come for me. Let me feel this pretty ass clench around my finger."

He thrust hard and fast before tensing and spurting hot and thick between our bellies. His body shuddered and his hole tightened around my finger. When Sage lay spent on top of me, spunk and lube cooling and sticky, I wrapped my arms around him. "That was fucking amazing. You're amazing. I don't care if that's as far as our sex life ever goes. It was beautiful and I could live the rest of my life doing just that."

Sage lifted his heavy, sated head to look in my eyes. "But you're on board with anal? I mean, I know some guys aren't. I'm okay with this too, if you don't want to go any further."

I kissed him. "I'm on board with anal if *you* are. If not, this and the other things we've done are perfectly fine for me."

"I'd like to try it. Maybe I won't like it, but I know I like to play with my ass with toys, so the thought of your cock inside me is a total turn-on." He kissed me back. "Shit, I never thought. Are you a top?"

I laughed. "Mostly. I've bottomed before and enjoyed it." I shrugged.

"Would you bottom for me?" Sage asked and bit his lip. "It's not something I've ever been super focused on doing, but the thought of you taking my cock has me thinking all sorts of sexy thoughts."

"I'd bottom for you in a heartbeat, no question." And it was the truth. With other guys, I'd been willing to switch things up from time to time for the fun of it, or if I somehow ended up with an exclusive top. But for Sage? Hell yes. My ass clenched at the thought of taking him.

"Mmm, so much fodder for my sexual fantasies." Sage cuddled into my chest and let me hold him for a bit longer.

"You want to see if the guys want to plan a lunch and arcade trip next Sunday?" I rubbed a hand up and down his back.

"Sounds perfect."

Perfect. He was right.

When was the last time anything in my life had been perfect?

Almost never.

Until I opened my heart and let this beautiful boy in.

12

SAGE

I WAS DOING that thing I never thought would happen for me. Smiling over a guy. Giddy about a guy. Heart aflutter about a guy. Not just any guy. Bode. One of my best friends. My protector, my contrast, my *boyfriend*, my lover.

Holy shit. I had a boyfriend.

Bode Silver was my boyfriend.

And I had two other best friends in the mix of a home and a job.

Benji and Kyson were totally in on going to lunch and the arcade.

We picked the next Sunday and the four of us had our guys' day out. We started at the 16-Bit Arcade and spent at least two hours playing vintage video games and sipping cocktails. Then we ended up over at Chatham Tap for lunch. The local English pub had an amazing atmosphere and between a Rueben sandwich, Italian sandwich, fish and chips, and a burger, the four of us were stuffed full by the time our bill arrived.

As we finished our food, Bode elbowed Kyson and said,

"Hey, isn't that one of the detectives we met when you had that booth at the local vendor event about a year ago?"

Kyson looked to where Bode was gesturing. "Yeah, I think it is. I don't remember his name off the top of my head, but I'm pretty sure he's one of the detectives we met along with several other officers."

Bode frowned. "I think it was Lewis or London or something similar to that."

Benji spoke up. "I wonder if he worked any of those cases around town where the bodies were found buried in cement."

Bode nodded. "I think he's one of the top detectives on the force, so he may have been involved in those cases. Maybe still dealing with them, not sure they've been solved."

After we paid our bill and were heading towards the door, Bode stopped by the detective's table. "Hi, I don't mean to interrupt your meal." Bode gestured toward the detective and the man who sat across from him. "My name is Bode Silver. I just wanted to say hello. We met about a year ago at a police-sponsored event. I don't expect you to remember me, but I wanted to thank you for your service on the force." Bode reached in his pocket and produced a business card. "Here's my card. I'm the owner of a new bar here on Mass. Ave. The Salty Lizard. If you're ever in the area looking for some drinks, music, and an open, friendly atmosphere, feel free to stop by. Drinks are on me."

The detective looked embarrassed, but shook Bode's hand and thanked him for the offer. The man across from Detective Lewis smiled and gave a small nod.

My heart soared at the simple act of kindness Bode had extended. His actions proved to me that behind that grumpy, gruff side was a good and loyal man. He was someone to be proud of. I looked forward to watching Bode grow and become the successful businessman he dreamed of being. And I wanted to stand by his side through it all.

* * *

"Would you be willing to have our pizza and movie date at Bay's place with Arlo rather than here by ourselves?" I gave Bode a pleading look. "Bay is stuck with no one to watch Arlo. Said he could take him to work, but I'd hate for the kid to have to sit at the shop if we're available to watch him." I frowned. "Or, I could just go watch him. You don't *have* to go."

Bode sidled up to my side at the kitchen counter and took my phone from me. He held it up for a photo with me and then pulled up Bay's name and sent the picture to him with a text saying, "We'll be there. Does Arlo like pepperoni?"

I grinned stupidly at him and wrapped my arms around his waist. "You're kinda amazing. You know that?"

"What? First, I wouldn't give up time with you unless I *have* to. Second, Arlo is a cool kid and I kinda love that the four of us can be part of making his life good after he lost his mom. Third, do you really think my stubborn, jealous ass would give up the chance to rub *us* in Bay's face?" Bode leaned in and kissed me softly.

"Bay isn't the least bit concerned about you and me, other than maybe to throw a *told you so* in your face." I wrinkled my nose. "I know Bay and Kyson both have a lot going on with their businesses and Bay is a new dad, but I kinda wish those two would just get together already."

"How do we know they haven't?"

"Well, I think both of them would be a lot less tense if they had; neither of them has that blissed-out look. And Kyson hinted that they both decided it would be best to get their businesses and Bay's personal life a little more settled before they explored anything between them." I shrugged. "I guess it's a grown-up type decision and all that. And they *do* need to consider Arlo."

"I like that kid, for real. Nothing like a child to make a person need to grow up. Without him, Bay and Ky could have avoided and denied and hidden from a relationship like we did." Bode smirked before he nuzzled my neck.

"Um, for the record, *you* did that all on your own. Don't go throwing me in that mess."

We headed to Bay's place.

I put in an order for pizza while we walked. Bay had replied to Bode's text with a selfie of him and Arlo saying the kid liked pepperoni just fine and that there were drinks at the apartment.

When Bay opened the door for us, Arlo peeked from behind his legs. He was usually quiet for a while until he got comfortable around new people. He settled in with me and the guys a lot more quickly now that we'd seen him more than a few times.

Within five minutes, Arlo had Bode in his room looking at a new toy.

Bay gave me a teasing smile. "I take it things are going well?"

I couldn't help the huge grin that filled my face. "Yeah, really well."

"The guys told me you two finally pulled your," he paused and cocked his head, "well, *Bode* finally pulled his head from his ass and realized you two would be good together."

I nodded, my cheeks flushed from thinking *how* good we were together.

"You taking it slow or just barreling ahead?" Bay wrote on a small notepad as he spoke.

"Figured we're both grown, we've spent a lot of time together getting to know each other without the pressures of a sexual relationship, so we're officially dating but not taking anything slowly." I waited for Bay to disapprove or give me shit.

But he didn't.

"Good for you. You guys already know each other well, you're living together, you're friends, no reason to waste time." He glanced toward Arlo's room where we could hear the little boy laughing. "Time isn't guaranteed."

My heart hurt for him. I knew he'd lost his sister and become a dad in the blink of an eye. That was a lot of overwhelming change. But did Bay's mind flit to Kyson the way mine did? It wasn't my place to say anything. Was it? But Kyson and Bay were dancing around each other as badly as Bode and I did. Maybe they needed a swift kick in the ass to see they were wasting time.

"No, it's not. Sometimes it's scary, but just jumping in and going for it is maybe best. Figure things out on the fly." I shrugged. Was I overstepping?

"Jump in and go for what?" Bay frowned.

I sputtered. "Whatever it is you are wanting."

Bay stared at me for a moment. "Well, I can't jump in the deep end anymore. I have 'Lo to think of. Spontaneity is fun, but it can also be masking poor choices and disasters waiting to happen."

Were we both referring to him and Kyson?

"Or it can be what you both need."

"What Arlo and I need?" Bay raised a brow.

"Maybe. Or maybe just what *you* need. Becoming a father doesn't have to hold you back. Raise Arlo to go after what he wants by modeling that for him." I checked my phone to see the pizza would arrive in about five minutes.

"Sometimes going after what you want *seems* like the right thing, but what if you're just lonely or having a midlife crisis?" Bay ran a hand over his face. "Or what if what you want doesn't want you back?"

My eyes went wide. "I can almost one hundred percent assure you that's not the case. But I'll stop crossing lines now and just go let the pizza guy in." I turned to head toward the door, but stopped and looked directly at Bay. "I know what it's like to be lonely. It's not like you'd be going after the first warm body you encountered. Taking it slow and letting yourself get settled isn't a bad idea, but don't get so comfortable with that excuse that you forget to let yourself live."

Bay smiled sadly and nodded.

When I returned with the pizza, Bay held up the little notebook. "Bedtime routine and times. Numbers other than mine if for some reason you can't get hold of me. Feel free to stream whatever you want on TV. There's beer, coffee, soda, and water. There's juice too but you'll have to fight Arlo for that."

I laughed and followed Bay to Arlo's room.

My heart caught in my chest when I saw Bode sitting on the floor playing with Arlo and his blocks. Three stuffed animals, a baby doll, and a dinosaur joined the fun.

"Hey, 'Lo. I'm going to head to work. You good with Sage and Bode?" Bay dropped to a knee to talk to his son.

Arlo nodded, smiled shyly at me, and then turned toward Bode with stars in his eyes. "Bye, Daddy," he said without even glancing Bay's way.

My heart was so full. The little boy had lost his mom, but he'd gained Bay as a father. From the tiny bit I knew, Bay's sister was a single mom and had really struggled with being a consistent and responsible mother for a lot of Arlo's short life. It made me sad the child had lost a parent, but I could tell Arlo loved Bay and was very well taken care of.

Bay gave Arlo hugs and kisses. "You listen when Sage and Bode say it's time for bed."

Arlo tugged on Bay's hand and pulled him close to whisper something.

Bay chuckled. "Well, I'm sure Sage and Bode would *love* to watch *Frozen* or *Paw Patrol* with you. Just brush your teeth first in case you fall asleep."

After Bay left, the three of us spent the next two hours eating pizza, playing with toys, and watching *Frozen*. Luckily, Arlo brushed his teeth and put on his pajamas before we switched to *Paw Patrol* because he was zonked out within the first ten minutes.

"Should we let him sleep here or take him to his bed?" Bode whispered as he glanced down at the little boy asleep between us.

Arlo's head was on Bode's lap, his legs across mine, and his thumb stuck in his mouth.

"Probably a lot more comfortable in his bed."

Bode nodded and slowly maneuvered himself to a standing position with Arlo in his arms.

The look of absolute concentration, abject fear, and sincere awe on Bode's face did strange things to my heart and stomach. He was terrified of messing something up with a sleeping kid in his arms, but he also comforted and cared for Arlo so naturally.

We tiptoed down the hallway. Bode was careful not to knock Arlo's head into the door frame. I turned on the moon nightlight just as Bay had instructed in his notes and pulled down the covers.

Arlo stirred in Bode's arms and we both froze. Bode swayed back and forth for a few minutes until the child settled again.

Bode walked toward the bed, stopped, and gave me a helpless look.

I raised my brow.

He gestured toward the bed with his chin. The pillow was to his left, but he was holding Arlo's head on his right arm.

I wrinkled my nose and tried to think of a solution. Before I came up with anything, Bode turned himself and sat on the bed. The new position put Arlo's head right at the pillow.

Bode placed the child onto the pillow and bed inch-by-inch and slowly wriggled his way out from the limp limbs. Once he stood, I pulled the covers over Arlo. We both stood for several moments, likely both holding our breaths, and watched to be sure he didn't wake up. Arlo shifted and made sleepy little noises. Bode and I froze and waited. When he didn't wake, we looked at each other and shrugged before sneaking quietly from the room.

Once we reached the living room, Bode flopped down on the couch and let out a long sigh. "Oh my God. That was nerve wracking. I was scared every move or breath was going to wake him."

I laughed and sat down to cuddle next to him. "You're amazing with him."

"Nah, just played with him and carried him like a bomb to bed."

I shook my head. "No, you've got a soft spot for him. Maybe for kids in general. And I loved watching you with him tonight. Made my heart all gooey." I kissed his neck, his cheek, and then nibbled at his ear. "My gruff guy has a heart of gold and is so very good with kids. Turns me the fuck on if you want to know the truth."

Bode turned fiery eyes my way. "Yeah?"

I nodded.

"May have to do something about that when I get you home." He brushed his lips against mine.

"Oh, there's no *may* about it." I teased his lips with my tongue.

He pulled back slightly and raised a brow.

"I've been playing with that butt plug and I've got it in tonight. You're going to take me home and fuck me long and hard until we both see stars."

Bode slow blinked before a sexy smile danced on his mouth and teased at his eyes. "I've got nothing, can't even argue with that plan. God, I can't believe you've had it in all night and didn't tell me." He kissed me slow and deep.

"Figured it wasn't appropriate topic of conversation while you played blocks with Arlo."

We both laughed and then spent the next hour curled on the couch pretending to watch a random movie until Bay came home. We bounded from the couch and out the door with Bay's knowing laughter behind us. I all but dragged Bode home and up the stairs.

* * *

"I want to take a quick shower, then we're going to bed for hours and hours." I kissed Bode's smiling mouth and shut the bathroom doors. As I climbed into the shower, I felt the water pressure dip slightly and figured Bode was taking a shower in the other bathroom.

I slowly slid the plug from my ass, cleaned it and my whole body, washed my hair, and all but jumped from the shower. I ran a towel haphazardly over my skin and rushed to Bode's room just as he walked in wrapped in a towel and locked the door behind him.

I crawled onto the bed before placing the sex toy on the side table and tossing lube and a condom next to it. Bode moaned and I smiled as I flopped my naked body back on the bed. My eyes were glued to Bode. He quirked his mouth and slowly let the towel drop from his waist.

Holy shit. He was so damn gorgeous. Long legs, dark smattering of hair all over, sinewy muscles in all the right places. A heavy cock protruding proudly. And all of it was mine, for me. Bode was mine. And I was his.

"We don't have to do anything you don't want to do." Bode placed a knee on the bed and moved toward me. "Are you having second thoughts?"

My brows shot up. "Only if you mean I've thought about you playing with my ass before you slide your long, thick cock deep into me."

Bode groaned as he wrapped me in his arms. "Killin' me." His mouth found mine and we kissed, hot and hard, for several moments. Our cocks rubbing together, hands trailing over damp skin, and chests heaving as the sexual anticipation in the room built. "Spread your legs."

I did as I was told, the cool air kissing my skin.

Bode retrieved the lube and butt plug. "Would you believe I've never played with one of these?"

My chest tightened. "So tonight can be a first for both of us."

Bode dropped the items and covered my body with his. He cupped my face in his hands. "I don't want this to be some cliché type situation. I need you to know I'm one hundred percent sure and being truthful. Not because of the sex, but because of you, because of us."

I frowned. "What are you talking about?"

Bode kissed me and leaned his forehead against mine. "I love you, Sage."

My sharp intake of breath reverberated in the room as his words did the same in my head and heart.

"I know it could seem like I'm just saying it for sex or it's too fast or whatever. But these are my true feelings for you. You're so damn important to me; it scares me how quickly you've become such a huge part of my life. But I wouldn't change it. I love you." Bode kissed me again.

My mouth opened for him and took his tongue deep before I pulled away, panting. "I love you too. So damn much."

We held each other tightly for a while before I cleared my throat.

"So, we love each other and all that. But what I'd *really* love right now is if you'd slide that thick plug in my ass and get me ready for your dick."

Bode growled and rolled off me. "Spread your legs again." He kissed my stomach, my groin, and my inner thighs before his lips brushed my balls. "Pull your legs back."

I hooked my arms behind my knees and spread myself wide for Bode.

When his lips whispered over my tight pucker, I caught my breath. Then his tongue teased my hole and I whimpered. The wet heat of his tongue and lips against my most sensitive area nearly brought sensory overload. He tongue fucked me until I thought I'd die, then reached for the lube and toy. Bode dribbled the slick liquid into my crack before preparing the plug.

I'd had the plug in on a few occasions and had stretched myself with it most of that day. But the stinging stretch as Bode pressed the tapered end slowly, slowly, slowly until the width increased and my body gave in and opened was breathtakingly beautiful.

"Fuck, Sage. Look at how you open for me." He kissed the skin of my ass cheek as he slowly plunged the plug in and out of my hole. "I can't wait until my cock slides deep in you."

I gasped. "Do it. Do it now, Bode, please. I want to feel you."

He pressed the toy deep a couple more times and seemed torn between teasing my ass or sinking his dick in deep. Bode tossed the plug to the side and grabbed the foil package. Tearing it open with his teeth, he rolled the condom down his cock. "How do you want to be?"

"I know I could probably control it better if I was on top, but I really want you over me, wrapping me in your arms." I spread my legs wider.

Bode knelt between my legs and pressed the head of his shaft against my hole. He inched in, my body offering only slight protest as he stretched me. Bode was a lot thicker and longer than the butt plug, but my ass adjusted to his invasion and we both sighed when he'd pushed himself completely inside me.

"Whoa," I whispered and took shallow breaths.

"You okay? Is it too much?"

I shook my head. "No, it's amazing. I feel so full, so complete."

Bode wrapped my legs around his waist and leaned down to kiss me as his arms engulfed me in a warm embrace. "You are so hot, so tight. You feel so damn good." He began to thrust slowly in and out.

I whimpered and held on tight. "I like this pace, but you can go harder and deeper."

He pulled out almost completely and my legs tightened around him before he surged hard and deep back into me.

"Oh God," I cried out.

Bode kissed me, capturing my whimpers and cries, as he continued to rock in and out. We fell into a slow, sensual rhythm and my balls tightened each time Bode's cock hit me deep inside.

"I need you to jack yourself. I'm not going to last and I need to see you come." Bode shifted and continued to thrust as he gripped my hips.

I took my throbbing cock in a fist and stroked to the same rhythm as Bode. I was torn between throwing my head back and losing myself to the sensations or watching my fist pump my cock as Bode fucked me. I couldn't tear my gaze away from the view so I watched every press of Bode's hips, the way his cock pulled out and slammed in. When Bode caressed my balls lightly, I lost any semblance of control I pretended to have. I squeezed my dick and groaned as sticky ropes spilled over my fist and splattered my stomach.

"Oh fuck," Bode hissed between clenched teeth as his cock erupted and pulsed.

We rode out our orgasms before Bode collapsed on top of me.

"Holy shit, is it always that good? I've gotten myself off plenty, but it's *never* been that good." I was still trying to catch my breath.

Bode attempted to lift himself on his elbows, but collapsed again. "No, not at all. Never been that good."

I winced as he pulled out. My body felt cold and empty.

Bode grabbed a t-shirt and wiped us both clean before discarding the condom. Within thirty seconds, he was back in bed and wrapping me in his arms.

"Can we do that again?" I snuggled against him.

"We can do that every day if you want." He kissed the top of my head. "You're fucking beautiful and amazing and I love you so damn much."

"Same. Thank you for being the person I got to share that with. I can't imagine anyone else taking my body in that way. I love you." My ass clenched thinking of what we'd just done.

Bode growled. "If I have my way, *no one* will ever have you that way except for me. This isn't just sex or a fling to me, Sage." He tightened his hold on me.

"It's not for me either. I want to belong to you. No one can complete me the way you do, no one can love me the way you do."

We fell into a well-sated sleep.

* * *

"I've got a project to finish and a test to study for, but I'll come down later to see if you need help." I stood leaning against the kitchen counter, legs spread, and arms wrapped around Bode's waist as he pressed against me, his arms around me with hands resting on the counter.

Every night of the past week had found us in Bode's bed, exploring each other's bodies, whispering our love words, and pretty much sucking or fucking each other's brains out. The sex was amazing, but the emotional connection that continued to grow stronger with each day was even more amazing.

Bode was having a lot of anxiety about the Lizard, profits, and his dad. He did a pretty good job keeping work and our relationship separated, but his nerves still showed through.

"You don't have to keep work stuff from me," I'd told him a couple days earlier. "I'm part of the bar, remember?" I bumped my hip against his. "Tell me when things are stressing you out."

He had sighed. "I just don't like bringing my dad's nastiness around you."

Now I nuzzled his neck and tried to figure out how to

push the work and studying I needed to do together so that I could get down to the bar and help even if just for a short while.

"Don't even stress it. Your project and test are both a lot more important than a couple hours in the bar. Probably won't even be that busy. Ky and Benji are both coming in to help, so we've got it covered." Bode kissed my neck, nibbled at my ear, and then captured my lips for a slow, teasing kiss. "Just have your work done in time for me to come to bed and ravish you."

I scoffed. "I feel like a kept man. Stuck in my room, only here for your sexual wants and wishes."

Bode started to chuckle, but then he pulled back and frowned. "You don't really feel that way do you? Because that's not at all…"

I laughed. "No, I'm totally joking."

Bode huffed a breath and whispered against my ear. "Good. Because my wants and wishes include fucking your gorgeous ass tonight."

I pressed the back of my hand to my forehead and sighed. "My services are never ending."

Bode hugged me and headed downstairs.

About fifteen minutes later, I heard Benji and Kyson coming up the stairs. I stuck around to chat with them for about ten minutes before beginning my school work.

Benji had been spending a lot of time at his temporary studio while final sale details were ironed out on his new building. I was pretty sure he'd been seeing someone too. Benji wasn't a player, but he also didn't have much history with stable relationships. From the little he'd said, and what Bode told me, Benji wanted a relationship that lasted more than a few hookups. But his fling guys either didn't want anything more serious, weren't right for anything more serious, or Benji talked himself out of anything potentially good before things could even get to that point.

Kyson was knee-deep in setting up Mass. Ave. Healing Massage and all that came with opening a business. I knew he was gaga over Bay, but neither man was willing or able to commit to anything at this time. Part of me thought Bode and I should watch Arlo so Bay and Kyson could at least burn up the sheets, but Kyson and Bay both seemed more like the relationship type than a quick hook-up type. And one night would likely be just the beginning of what they wanted with each other. Kyson's business life wasn't going to get any easier any time soon, and Bay was now a father with all the responsibilities that came with loving and raising a child. I'd keep my nose out of it.

"You coming down later?" Benji took a long sip of water.

I shrugged. "Bode said not to bother since I have a project and test. Said it probably wouldn't be super busy."

Benji glanced at Kyson who raised a brow but quickly schooled his features.

"Yeah, probably good to get school work done. That comes first." Kyson slapped me on the back.

"You guys holler if you get swamped, okay? I figure Bode is too stubborn to ask for help."

The look that passed between Kyson and Benji a second time wasn't my imagination, but I wasn't sure what it could have meant. I let it go and headed to my room. Project first. Then studying. If, and *only* if, I got to a point in studying where I felt completely confident in the material, I'd go downstairs and see if they needed me for anything. If not, I knew the guys could handle it. And Bode would be up to bed before I knew it.

* * *

Three hours later, I was done. I couldn't have studied anymore even if I wanted to. I slammed books, notebooks, and my laptop shut. Standing from my desk chair, my back popped as I stretched and moaned. I slipped out my earbuds and heard the music that went along with the rhythmic bass that had thumped through the floor and kept me company while I worked.

I checked my phone. No messages. But there was still time to help. I drank a bottle of water and took some pain reliever for a headache I felt coming on. Too much being bent over my keyboard; I needed to see Kyson for a massage. After washing my face and peeing, I ran down the back stairs. I was beyond ready for a break and to spend some time with my friends.

I made sure the back room wasn't in total disarray before heading to the front.

One glance around the place allowed for a quick assessment. The place was packed. The bar line was massive. Food orders looked backed up. Tables needed cleaned and reset. Glasses were running low. Benji, Kyson, and Bode looked as if they were being run ragged.

What the fuck? Why didn't they call me?

And then I saw him.

Dick Silver.

Bode had lied to me.

My heart lurched and twisted with pain.

But the smarmy look on Dick Silver's face sparked an

anger that temporarily covered the hurt. I gritted my teeth and made a decision. Without a second thought as to *why* Bode hadn't wanted me in the bar, I went into *step it up* mode and pitched in to help.

I cleared and reset tables.

Then restocked glasses.

Then helped clear the bar line.

Then went to the kitchen to help fill orders.

About forty-five minutes later, the music continued thumping, tables were filled with people eating and drinking, the dance floor was filled, and I could finally take a breath.

I glanced toward Dick and did my best to not roll my eyes as he sat sipping what I'd bet was our priciest scotch, smiling smugly as he looked down his nose.

I tossed the towel I'd been using to dry glasses in a bucket and went to the back room. I needed to take a moment to clear my head and gather my thoughts.

A few moments later, I heard Bode's office door open.

Then voices.

Then yelling.

Then the door slammed shut.

13

BODE

THE MOMENT I'd been dreading was here.

And I'd made it a thousand times worse by lying to Sage. I saw the moment he'd entered the bar and realized *why* I'd urged him not to come downstairs tonight.

But then my heart tumbled deeper in love with him when he pitched in and helped us out of a massive busy rush. Sage hadn't even hesitated.

I'd lied to him. I'd seen his wounded eyes.

Yet he fucking *helped* when I knew he was furious. And hurt.

I didn't deserve him.

And then my dad started in on me.

He'd been threatening to come to The Salty Lizard since opening night. I'd known he'd show up at some point. I was actually surprised I got a couple hours' notice. I doubt Dick had meant for me to know about his visit, but Mom had let it slip when Benji had spoken to her earlier in the day.

The moment I knew Dad was on his way, my stomach

roiled and tied itself in knots. The night would be busy, but we were well-prepared as with any night. I wouldn't have purposefully *asked* Sage to stay away, but the fact that he had a ton of homework gave me the perfect avenue to protect him from my father. Dad wasn't coming for a friendly visit. He was coming to threaten, breathe down my neck, put some fear into me, assert his dominance. I knew he'd be in full Dick Silver mode. My chest burned at the thought of putting Sage anywhere near that toxicity.

But my sweet boy was too good and pushed aside his needs to help the guys and me.

And caught me in a lie. Perhaps a lie of omission, but a lie nonetheless.

I'd seen a flash of angry Sage disappear to the back room and started to follow.

Only to be stopped by Dad.

"Not sure this is an establishment I want my money tied up in." Dick moved slowly to halt my progress toward Sage. "Perhaps we should discuss how I see this playing out in the office."

I clenched my teeth and nodded.

When Dick attempted to walk to the office in front of me, I shouldered myself slightly in front of him with a double step. No way he was going to lead the way to *my* office.

With a longing glance toward the back room door on the left, I turned right and opened my office door.

Dad barged in and stood to the side of my desk as if trying to gain the upper hand. Ten years ago, five years ago, hell maybe even two years ago, I would have likely physically and emotionally cowered to his bullish ways. But not now. Not when I had my dream in my sights. He was part of it financially, but I wouldn't allow him to walk all over me. I made a split decision that no matter how the conversation went down, my first priority was to make things right with Sage and then figure a way to buy out my dad's investment in The Salty Lizard.

"Well, that was a sad disappointment on many levels," Dad drawled. He'd been drinking, but he wasn't in a mellow mood, he was in a fighting mood.

There were so many things I could have said. *A big crowd wasn't expected tonight. Being busy like that is a positive. New hire's paperwork wasn't finalized just yet.* But they all sounded like excuses even to my ears. So, I crossed my arms and narrowed my eyes. "How long do you plan to hang your control of this place over my head?"

Dick's face registered surprise for a flitting moment before switching to anger. "Excuse me?"

"I'm just wondering how long I can expect you to try to bully me with your money."

"I *own* this place. My name is on the line. I have every right to expect it to run smoothly and make money." His face reddened as his voice rose. "You've always been too weak. Pardon me for demanding that my investment is sound and that this place is run by a professional business mind."

I stalked to the door and slammed it shut with slightly more force than I'd meant to. "This place is running fine." I attempted to keep my voice down, but the anger raised my volume. "We're in the black and our numbers predict a continued profit. I've shared all of this with you. So, what's the point of you even being here? Want to come share in our success? Celebrate with us? Bring Mom? Great! But if you're just coming to glare and bully and try to intimidate, you're not welcome. Investment or not." I pinched the bridge of my nose before focusing on Dad's flushed and angry face. "I appreciate the loan—which, by the way, you said you'd give me a year to prove this place could be a success—but if you're going to dangle it over my head as a way of keeping me under your thumb, I'll look into alternate options. I'm thirty-four fucking years old. Your *help* is welcome and needed. Your control and threats are *not*."

Dad drained the rest of his scotch. "You've always let your emotions lead you around by the balls. Even the dumbest of business owners know that you're only as good as your staff. Any idiot could see that you were understaffed tonight. A big crowd is great *if* you can serve them and keep them happy. Give them bad service and you'll lose them."

"Had a new guy supposed to start tonight, but his paperwork isn't finalized. I'm not going to risk having him work without everything being legit. Benji, Kyson, and I were handling it fine. We just got slammed for a bit." An image of Sage flitted through my brain, warmed my heart, and worried me all at the same time.

"You're lucky that twink of a renter you've got showed up to help."

I was across the room in less than two seconds. Hands fisted in Dad's shirt, I pressed him against the wall. "Don't *ever* talk about Sage that way."

Dick's eyes narrowed before taking on an evil gleam. "He seems like a good worker. He saved your ass by showing up when he did and stepping in to help. Maybe you should take business advice from him rather than just letting him suck your dick."

I dropped my hands, took a step back, and swung my arm back.

"Stop. He's not worth it." Sage's soft voice was strong and his warm hand held my arm. He let my arm drop and stepped in front of me to face my dad who was smoothing his hands down his rumpled shirt. "Mr. Silver, you disgust me and I'm so glad that your son grew up to be the exact opposite of you. You'd be lucky to have a sliver of his work ethic, his drive and determination, or his people skills. Bode is a good and kind man, a hard worker to the point of overdoing it, and has brilliant plans for this bar. I'd place money that every single customer tonight will be back and will bring friends. Even before I stepped in to help with the rush, I'd venture to say a vast majority would have been coming back. Why? Because The Salty Lizard is a place where people feel welcome and wanted. It's a place where the food and drinks are great, but the atmosphere and socializing are even better. Why? Because of Bode. He's made this place a success in a very short time. You and I both know the numbers don't lie. The Lizard is a success and is on track for nothing but more of the same." Sage stepped closer and took his voice down a couple notches. "You're wasting your time coming here trying to assert your power, but go ahead if it makes you happy. We welcome you watching this place soar. Maybe someday you'll admit that Bode is a better person than you can ever hope to be and is a screaming success in every damn way that even comes close to mattering."

My dad sneered. "Cute. Got a little yapper coming to your defense, huh?" He glanced between Sage and me. "Nice speech. But the fact remains, I own part of this place with the amount of money I loaned you. I have every right to be sure my money is being spent wisely and I plan to do just that. Whenever I want. I don't like what I see? I'll pull my money." He shrugged. "I'll see myself out." Dick sauntered from the office.

A heavy silence hung in the office.

I took a deep breath and turned to Sage. "Thank you for your help tonight. For standing up for me just now." My heart began to beat again when Sage walked into my arms and snuggled against my chest. My arms wrapped around him and never wanted to let go. "I don't deserve you. I'm sorry for tonight."

Sage breathed deeply against my chest and then backed away. "I love you. But I've got some things to say."

I nodded. I'd known it was coming. I would have been worried if Sage didn't lay into me. But it wasn't going to be fun.

He pressed a finger against my chest. "You *lied* to me. After I told you that being lied to, deceived, kept out of the loop are things I despise—things my parents did to screw with me and fuck me up—you lied." Sage's voice wavered and his face crumpled.

My chest hurt and tears stung my eyes. "Sage, I'm sorry. I found out earlier he was coming. I knew it wouldn't be pretty. I never would have purposely asked you to stay away, but knowing you had a lot of work to do made me think I could keep you away from him." I reached for his hand and held it against my chest. "All I wanted to do was protect you from him."

A tear ran down Sage's cheek. "When I walked in tonight and saw you were swamped and *needed* my help, but you kept me away, all I could think was that you were embarrassed by me. Or didn't want your dad seeing us together. Or that I wasn't good enough to help you prove your success to your dad. It felt like you were keeping me hidden away. Like I'm only good enough for certain parts of your life." His voice cracked and he sobbed as I pulled him against my chest.

"Sage, no." I kissed the top of his head and held him tight. "Don't ever think that. I was wrong for keeping the truth from you, but in my fucked up head it meant protecting you from him." I rubbed his back as his tears soaked my shirt. "Dick Silver is toxic and he seems to be more so these days. I think maybe it has to do with the fact that I don't roll over and let him walk all over me like I used to. He seems to be desperate and lashing out more and more. Tonight was as bad as I feared it would be. I just didn't want you exposed to him, didn't want him tainting you with his hatred of me."

Sage took a deep shuddery breath. "I can see that now. He was terrible. But all of my insecurities came bubbling to the surface when I figured out you'd kept me away. I wish you'd just asked me to avoid the bar so that I didn't have to be around Dick."

I chuckled. "Because you would have done that?"

Sage pulled back and looked at me before sniffing and grinning. "Hell no. But I would have at least known the real reason for why you didn't want me down there instead of letting my imagination go wild."

I dipped my head and kissed him softly. "I love you and I'm so sorry for making you feel that way. My heart was in the right place, but I handled it the wrong way."

"Did the guys know you didn't want me down there?"

I winced. "They figured it out after talking to you. They both chewed my ass when they got down here. Said I was making a mistake and should've been honest with you."

"They are wise, wise men." Sage winked and stood on his tiptoes to kiss me. "I can see how this situation was a mistake and misplaced protection led to hurt feelings. But don't ever lie to me again. I can't be in a relationship where I'm not treated with respect and honesty."

I swallowed thickly and nodded. "I will *always* want to protect you, but I'll never lie to make it happen. I'm sorry."

Sage snuggled his cheek against my chest. "Your dad is an absolute dick."

We both chuckled.

"Yes, yes he is."

We stood wrapped in each other's arms for several moments.

"Oh God, the things I said to him. I'll never be invited to holidays." Sage groaned.

I laughed. "Mom would never let that happen. And if you're not invited, I don't go either."

"Same here," Benji spoke from the doorway.

"Our moms will never not invite us, but if Dick and Rod want to be assholes, the four of us stay home and make our own traditions." Kyson leaned against the door frame.

"Well, if it comes to that, we should definitely invite Janet and Debbie up here to celebrate with us." Sage smiled toward Benji and Kyson before resting his head on my chest again.

"What happened back here?" Benji asked. "Dick left pissed and in a hurry."

"He started in on me about how much I suck and how

he owns this place and he can destroy me, blah, blah, blah." I shifted Sage to my side and held him close. "But Sage barged in and gave him a tongue lashing the likes of which I'm pretty sure Dick Silver has never experienced. He made a few disparaging remarks and threats then he left." I sighed. "I'm not going to lie. I'm scared to death he's going to take the bar from me."

Sage put his arm around my waist. "I say we put a plan into motion to make sure that doesn't happen."

Benji and Kyson smiled.

"I like the way your boy thinks, Bo." Kyson winked.

"Let's get out of here. We got everything cleaned up." Benji gestured toward the backdoor. "Sage, thanks for saving our asses tonight. We told this big lug he was making a bad decision not telling you about Dick. Glad you came down anyway. Sorry you got hurt." Benji waggled his brows. "I would have *loved* to hear you lay into Dad."

Sage groaned. "It wasn't pretty. I can't believe I said most of it."

"Love makes you do crazy things." Kyson shrugged.

We headed up the stairs as I filled the guys in on all that had gone on and been said in the office.

We all said goodnight, showered, and headed to bed. The apartment was dark and still. Exhaustion was setting in after the emotional turmoil the night had brought.

Sage crawled into my bed—the only bed I ever wanted to see him in again—and lay face down in the middle.

"Hey, you okay?" I asked as I flipped off the bathroom light and tossed my towel on the chair. I crawled onto the bed and lay beside him.

Sage shivered as my naked heat warmed his skin. I

trailed my hand over his skin caressing his shoulders, his back, his waist before I cupped his bare ass.

"I need you," he whispered.

"You seem like you're about to sleep like the dead."

"Please," Sage begged. "Inside me. We'll sleep, but I need to feel you fill me, complete me."

Without another word, I reached into the bedside table for a condom and lube.

"Let me suck you." Sage turned his head toward me and opened his beautiful mouth as he pushed up on his elbows.

I groaned as I watched my cock slip between his pink lips. He licked and sucked and tongued me until I was rock hard and ready for his ass. I moved to straddle his legs, tore open the condom and rolled it on. I slicked my dick with lube and coated Sage's crack before teasing a finger in his tight hole.

"Don't need prep, just need you." Sage lifted his ass slightly, arching his back.

"I don't want to hurt you."

"Won't. Just go slow. Fuck me hard and slow."

I gripped Sage's hips and lifted so his ass spread slightly. Lining my thick head up with his body, I pressed gently against his pucker. Sage's hot hole hugged me tightly as I entered him inch by fucking inch until he took me completely. My body covered Sage's and I murmured in his ear, "You're so fucking tight, so damn beautiful, I love you."

Sage seemed to fight against exhaustion to turn his head and kiss me. "Long, deep, slow strokes. Fuck me, love me, make me yours."

I hooked my arms under his armpits and held him as

my hips plunged long and slow into his prone body. My height and width covered Sage as my dick thrust between his lubed cheeks, his body engulfing my every stroke.

Sage whimpered and clenched the sheets. "Come in me. Please, I need to feel you empty inside me."

I moaned and increased my thrusts. "I'm going to fill your gorgeous ass and then I'm going to suck your cock until you shoot down my throat."

The shiver that traveled through Sage was my undoing. My balls drew up tight and I slammed my dick deep before unloading pulse after throbbing pulse.

Sage protested when I pulled out, but I quickly tossed the condom before rolling him to his side. I nestled into the bed with my mouth right at his hard, leaking cock. "Fuck my face."

Sage moaned as his cock slid between my lips and deep into my throat.

I gripped his ass and encouraged him to thrust harder.

As Sage fucked my mouth, I teased his balls and pressed a finger into his still slick hole.

He cried out and spilled in my mouth, spurting hard and hot in the back of my throat.

After I cleaned us both up, I took Sage in my arms and pulled the covers over us.

"You okay?" I whispered.

"I'm good. Today was hard. But I love you and I trust you," Sage mumbled.

"I'll spend the rest of my life proving to you that you are worthy of respect and trust." My voice caught on the words, but I meant them to my very soul.

"And I'll give you the rest of my life to prove it." His words were thick with sleep. "As long as I get to prove to you how brilliant and successful you are." He paused so long I thought he'd fallen asleep, but then he sighed and snuggled deeper against me. "We've got a damn bright future ahead of us."

I fell asleep with Sage wrapped in my arms, my heart content and in love, and the image of our future dancing in my head.

EPILOGUE
SAGE

SIX WEEKS *Later*

I winked at Kyson as I picked up Bode's phone and carried it to the kitchen.

"Hey, babe? You got a text." I pretended to squint at the screen. "From the bank?" I stopped walking and frowned. "Oh, loan application failed?"

Bode's face fell.

I laughed. "I'm kidding. There's no text." I handed him his phone and wrapped my arms around his waist. "With caller ID the way it is, it's hard as hell to set up a prank call these days. So, consider that as close to a prank as I'll ever get." I kissed Bode's cheek.

Bode sighed. "That was mean. So mean. You're lucky I love you." He kissed me, tracing my lips with his tongue and dipping in slightly to meet mine.

"You already got the preliminary approval, I don't think your application is going to fall through." I kissed him once more before moving away to grab a box of cereal and pour two bowls.

The week after Dick had visited the Lizard, Bode sat down with all of us and asked for our input on getting a loan. He'd saved some money already from the Lizard's profits, he had the numbers to show the bar was making money, and he had excellent credit. The four of us agreed that owing the bank would be stressful, but it would be less stressful than owing Dick.

Bode took time to weigh his options and rethink the decision, but in the end, after a couple weeks of thinking it over, he opted to apply for a loan. The fact that Dick had been making thinly veiled threats again probably helped him make the decision.

The loan officer had seemed very sure that the amount Bode was asking for—which was just slightly over what he owed Dick—would be approved easily. Bode was expecting the final approval any day now.

Bode and I were solid in our relationship. Once he admitted there was something between us, he went full speed ahead and never looked back. I'd moved into his room completely and we'd discussed the possibility of taking in a new renter.

"Yeah, but we don't *need* the extra rent money." Benji had wrinkled his nose.

"And we honestly lucked out big time with Sage. Do we want to risk taking in another renter?" Kyson scrunched up his face.

"Maybe one of you two could find the love of your life in the new renter like I did with Sage." Bode enjoyed teasing the guys, but he had also taken to laughing at himself over how much he tried to fight what everyone else had been able to see between us.

Now, as Kyson, Bode, and I sat at the table eating

cereal and chatting, we heard Benji's door open. Expecting to see Benji's dark hair, the three of us nearly choked on our cereal when a blond head with glasses and a scruffy beard darted past and out the door.

Benji's red face appeared, but he made for the kitchen as if we weren't going to discuss that last night's hookup had just done the walk of shame past us.

"Who was that?" Bode asked with a smirk and followed Benji to the kitchen as he continued to shovel cereal in his mouth.

"Just a guy." Benji took a long drink of water.

"One nighter?"

Benji flushed. "We've seen each other a couple times."

"Is it serious?" Kyson asked his cousin.

I ate my cereal and watched the exchange like I was at a tennis match.

"No. Sex is amazing, but we're not a great match. He's a few years older. Starting a business of his own. We're both artists, so we'd likely be at each other's throats competing over our work." Benji finished his water. "Sorry about the exit. We overslept. Planned to have him out before you guys were up and about. I suggested he stay and at least say hi, but he had somewhere he had to be."

Interesting that Benji would want a *nothing serious* guy to meet us.

But it wasn't my business.

"Well, if it turns into more, we'd love to meet him."

"What's his name?" I piped up as I stood to carry my bowl to the kitchen.

"Rhys." Benji blushed and bit his lip.

Whether he wanted to admit it or not, he liked this

Rhys guy. Would two artists really butt heads over their work? I shrugged it off internally. Again. Not my business.

Benji's phone rang.

"Hello?" He paused and listened. "Yes." Pause. "Yeah, that will work fine." Pause. "Looking forward to it." Pause. "Yeah, you too. Thanks. See you then."

When he hung up, Benji turned a huge grin our way. "That was my realtor. Says I should come down to the new building today and sign some final paperwork."

We all whooped and slapped him on the back.

"About fucking time." Bode pulled his brother in for a hug.

Benji sighed and ran a hand over his face. "I've been waiting so long to have a studio and place of my own. I'm tired of renting shared studio space. I want to be able to create, teach, and sell all in one location. The Silver Creative is one step closer to reality."

Two hours later, the four of us trooped down the stairs and walked a few blocks to where Benji's new building was located. It was an older space, but it had been completely renovated and both the exterior and interior were spectacular.

We entered the building and were greeted by Benji's realtor, Kris. She frowned.

"What's up? Something fall through?" Benji returned her serious expression.

"Well, it appears there's been a bit of a snafu the likes of which I've never dealt with."

Benji crossed his arms over his chest and scowled just as the door opened and two people walked in.

A flash of blond hair caught my eye.

Rhys? Why would a *nothing serious* guy be at Benji's closing?

"What are you doing here?" Benji demanded.

"Could ask you the same thing." Rhys stopped and looked at his realtor. She shrugged.

Another person entered the front door. An older man who looked nervous.

"Ah, yes. Well, I see we're all present and accounted for." The man wrung his hands. "I must say, this is not something I have experience with, but I'm sure we can get it all worked out. Just some miscommunication, I'm sure."

"What's the problem?" Rhys asked.

"Well, it appears that both a Mr. Rhys Golden *and* a Mr. Benjamin Silver have leased this building." The older man grimaced. "An interesting and unfortunate predicament, but one I'm most sure we can set to right."

Almost everyone's mouths dropped open.

Rhys frowned.

Benji frowned.

Bode whistled.

Well, this was going to be interesting.

* * *

Want more of the guys from Silver in the City? Check out book 2, <u>Silver & Gold</u> coming January 20, 2020! getbook.at/SilverGold

Find other great books by A.D. Ellis at https://www.amazon.com/A.D.-Ellis/e/B00K0YJ8CW

Discover freebies at https://www.adellisauthor.com

Newsletter sign-up
https://www.subscribepage.com/
ADEllisNewsMMRomance

NOTES

If you've never been to Indy (Indianapolis, Indiana) you should definitely check out the places mentioned in the story!

16-Bit Bar and Arcade- http://www.16-bitbar.com/indy
Global Gifts- https://www.globalgiftsft.com/
Mass. Ave. Wine- http://massavewine.com/
Pumkinfish- https://pumkinfish.com/
Silver in the City- https://www.silverinthecity.com/
Rooster's Kitchen- http://roostersindy.com/
Chatham Tap- http://chathamtap.com/

ACKNOWLEDGMENTS

It's always so hard to write this part because I'm worried I'll forget someone without meaning to.

Readers- you are the reason I write. As long as you continue reading my stories, I'll continue writing them. Thank you for your support.

Bloggers- your support, reviews, and promotion are very much appreciated. Thank you!

My author buddies- I don't know that I could keep doing this without our brainstorm sessions, laughter, road trips, meals, wine, and friendship as my support.

Thank you to my betas, editors, proofreaders, and ARC readers! Your eyes and input are beyond important to me.

Brett and Gage- as usual, I doubt you even grasp how much your support, input, and friendship mean to me. This author journey has brought many wonderful things into my life, and you both are two of the BEST! I'm blessed to call you friends.

My family and friends- thank you for your love and support, always.

ABOUT THE AUTHOR

A.D. Ellis is an Indiana girl, born and raised. She spends much of her time in central Indiana as an instructional coach/teacher in the inner city of Indianapolis, being a mom to two amazing school-aged children, and wondering how she and her husband of almost two decades have managed to not drive each other insane. A lot of her time is also devoted to phone call avoidance and her hatred of cooking.

She loves chocolate, wine, pizza, and naps along with reading and writing romance. These loves don't leave much time for housework, much to the chagrin of her husband. Who would pick cleaning the house over a nap or a good book? She uses any extra time to increase her fluency in sarcasm.

Find all of Ellis' contemporary romance and male/male romance at www.adellisauthor.com

FREE books-- sign up at bit.ly/ADEllisNews for a FREE male/female romance.

Sign up at http://www.subscribepage.com/ADEllisNewsMMRomance for a FREE male/male romance book.

www.ingramcontent.com/pod-product-compliance
Lightning Source LLC
Chambersburg PA
CBHW020812060726
47498CB00017B/2764